Renzo's brain told him to be careful

Too bad his instinctive side was already caught up in the soft flame of Esme's embrace and the unmistakable message of her lips planted against his. How could he interpret the signs as anything but a blinking neon-green light?

Breaking away from the liquid fire of her kiss, Renzo sought confirmation. He needed her to make the call tonight, since she had pushed him away last time.

"What is it you want, Esmerelda? I need to be sure."

"I want the kind of pleasures you started to give me the other night," she whispered. His body reacted immediately, an automatic spike of temperature between them.

"You like the way I touched you?" He trailed a hand down her hip, stretched his fingers across her thigh. His thumb pressed into the soft flesh, eliciting a throaty hum from the back of her throat.

"Yes. I liked it too much." Her restless hands moved over him, sending those rising temperatures into the red-hot zone

"Esme, there's no such thing as liking it too much."

Dear Reader,

SINGLE IN SOUTH BEACH meets THE WRONG BED miniseries…oh, the possibilities! What a glamorous backdrop, and I already had the perfect hero in mind, since one of the owners of Club Paradise has a slew of gorgeous, overprotective brothers. I couldn't wait to put one of them in the path of an unsuspecting female to see what happened!

The result is *One Naughty Night,* a classic case of an immovable object colliding with an irresistible force. I loved watching the way Esmerelda Giles learns to work around this particular immovable man, Renzo Cesare!

I hope you'll join me for a very special SINGLE IN SOUTH BEACH story coming in January 2004. Look for *Valentine Vixen* in a volume entitled *Strangers in Paradise* with author Stephanie Bond. And there will be more SINGLE IN SOUTH BEACH books in spring 2004.

Visit me at www.JoanneRock.com to learn about future releases or to let me know what you think about the series!

Happy reading,

Joanne Rock

Books by Joanne Rock

HARLEQUIN TEMPTATION
863—LEARNING CURVES
897—TALL, DARK AND DARING
919—REVEALED

*Single in South Beach

HARLEQUIN BLAZE
26—SILK, LACE &
        VIDEOTAPE
48—IN HOT PURSUIT
54—WILD AND WILLING
87—WILD AND WICKED
104—SEX & THE SINGLE
        GIRL*
108—GIRL'S GUIDE TO
        HUNTING & KISSING*

JOANNE ROCK

ONE NAUGHTY NIGHT

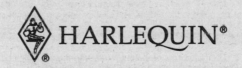

HARLEQUIN®

TORONTO • NEW YORK • LONDON
AMSTERDAM • PARIS • SYDNEY • HAMBURG
STOCKHOLM • ATHENS • TOKYO • MILAN • MADRID
PRAGUE • WARSAW • BUDAPEST • AUCKLAND

For the fantastic community readers at eHarlequin.com—thank you so much for the shared support, encouragement and twenty-four-hour entertainment. Also, I'd like to invite new readers and writers to join us. I'm often in the Blaze Boudoir or at the Temptress Tales thread on the Books & Authors board, but I bet you'll find lots of other great chats to enjoy, as well!

ISBN 0-373-69151-3

ONE NAUGHTY NIGHT

BAD DECISION number five thousand thirty-eight—overdressing.

Esmerelda Giles rocked back on the low heels of her sandals and sighed as she watched the parade of half-clad bodies strut down Ocean Drive toward the swanky new dance club that would be her destination tonight.

Even though the hands on her antique silver-and-turquoise watch pointed to 11:32 p.m., the well-lit street hummed with activity. A steady stream of cars rolled down the avenue at a snail's pace to see and be seen. Foot traffic converged on Club Paradise from every direction as if all of South Beach wanted a chance to meet and mingle at Miami's most risqué hot spot.

And every single person Esme laid eyes on wore considerably less than she did.

Shoot. How could she have made such a mistake after spending at least forty-five minutes deciding what to wear for this ridiculous blind date?

Esme fingered the featherweight silk of her outfit—a vintage gypsy dress she'd unearthed at a consignment shop on one of her antiquing outings. The gossamer garment ranked as the most seductive item of clothing she'd ever owned, yet it looked like a school-girl's frock next to the sexy getups sported by every woman in line at Club Paradise's side entrance across the street.

Once again, Esme's judgment had been faulty.

Surprise, surprise.

In the weeks since she'd lost her job, her car, a little bit of her self-respect and her life's dream to boot, Esme had been trying really hard not to exercise her own judgment. In fact, following the explosion of her previously well-ordered life, she'd realized that every decision she'd ever made had led her to lose her job, her car, some self-respect and her life's dream. There-fore, she couldn't trust her horrendous instincts.

Which accounted for her new desire to do the *opposite* of everything her instincts suggested.

She would have never considered going on a blind date before, but now as she waded through the rubble of her old existence, she'd decided maybe she ought to try it. She'd accepted her kindly new neighbor's matchmaking attempt and had agreed to meet the woman's nephew at the Moulin Rouge Lounge inside Club Paradise tonight.

Yippee.

While she stood on the street corner where the bus had deposited her and debated what to do about her overdressed condition, Esme was jostled by a pack of young men. She stepped aside quickly, mindful that she needed to quit dreaming and pay attention to her surroundings. A tall guy with spiky hair and a red silky T-shirt swept past her making breathy little *psst* sounds at her in the way one might call to an animal.

Is this how people communicated attraction these days, or was the man trying to insult her with his cat-call? God, she was so out of touch with the real world. She hadn't been on a genuine date since grad school and even then she'd only gone out with history geeks who were as socially inept as her.

But no more.

Tonight marked a symbolic change in Esme's life. A new mode of thinking, a new take-charge attitude. She'd thought the way to keep her touchy-feely former boss at bay was by buttoning up to the gills in conservative suits and layers of clothes, but Mr. Too Many Hands had probably read her insecurities in her wardrobe and thought he could help himself.

Steam hissed through her as she remembered those moments trapped in his grip and the ugly fallout of her resistance. She'd been fired in short order for sexual harassment even though *he* had been the one harassing *her*. Using his techno-nerd skills, her ex-boss had managed to manipulate the company computer system into printing out manufactured obnoxious e-mails supposedly from her to him. And now here she stood a week later

Pissed and unemployed.

But ready to make a few changes in her life.

Stepping back into the shadows of an alleyway between two of South Beach's historic, ice-cream-colored art deco buildings, Esme decided to make a few last minute adjustments to her wardrobe before she embarked on her blind date. The little overnight bag she planned to drop off in her complimentary hotel room before her midnight rendezvous didn't include a change of clothes other than the casual outfit she'd wear tomorrow.

And frankly, she didn't even want to cross over to that swanky, sexy side of the street looking like she did right now. She couldn't do much about overdressing since she had no intention of stripping off her dress. But ditching another item of clothing might make her feel a little more daring and a lot more naked.

Reaching beneath her blouse, Esme unhooked her white lacy bra and wriggled out of the straps one arm at a time. Her barely-34Bs didn't really require the support and somehow going braless seemed even more bold than baring a little midriff.

Old Esme never would have taken such a risk. New Esme planned to do just the opposite.

Flinging her bra off to one side to drape across a stainless steel trash can, Esmerelda Giles prepared to meet her blind date—one Mr. Hugh Duncan, journalist—with a serious take-charge attitude.

And possibly a little jiggle.

"Renzo, no woman is ever going to snap you up with that kind of old-fashioned attitude." Giselle Cesare, head chef at Club Paradise and part owner of the popular singles playground, stirred her teriyaki sauce and glared at her older brother.

"Since when has it been my mission in life to get snapped up?" Renzo stood propped in the half-open door shortly before the resort's main kitchen closed for the night and stared out over the writhing, wriggling bodies on the dance floor of the Moulin Rouge Lounge. He reached behind him to poke his mouthy sister in the ribs and steal a hunk of bread from the crusty Tuscan loaf sliced on the counter beside her. "I'm swearing off women since Celeste anyhow, remember?"

He'd been engaged to a woman raised as old-school Italian as him, but even *she'd* gotten scared off at the last minute by the idea of lifelong commitment. According to Celeste, she couldn't allow her first lover to be her last.

Not that he blamed her exactly, but he sure as hell would have liked to have been informed of her decision before he showed up at the altar in his tux.

No, he definitely wasn't in any hurry to be snapped up by any one right now. He shoved his pilfered bread in his mouth and resumed watching the erotic flow of scantily clad bodies out on the dance floor. Still leaning in the doorway, he could easily monitor the activity outside the room while occasionally helping Giselle with her work in the kitchen. Even after all formal food service ceased at midnight, the main kitchen still buzzed with activity until almost dawn thanks to twenty-four hour room service and the prep work that needed to be done before the hotel's three restaurants opened for breakfast.

Despite the high titillation factor of the action in the lounge, Renzo wasn't here to take in the floor show. He usually spent his few evenings away from his carpentry work at Club Paradise in order to keep an eye on his baby sister, although tonight there was an added chore. Later he needed to meet his older brother Nico to discuss the Cesare family finances and how in the hell they were going to cover their little brother's law school expenses without going broke. Renzo was already working every spare second of the day. He needed to figure out a way to channel a more high-end product to a higher-paying clientele, but so far he hadn't come up with how to accomplish this.

"Oh please. Renzo Cesare the monk?" Giselle ladled her sauce over a fresh batch of spinach noodles and slivers of grilled chicken. "Don't try and tell me you're swearing off women. It's been six months since Celeste went back to Rome. Move on already."

"And you're such an expert on heartbreak, Ann Landers?" Renzo hadn't mentioned his new financial concerns to Giselle, knowing his sister felt guilty enough about spending her inheritance by investing in Club Paradise. And although the idea of Giselle opening her own business where she could indulge the full extent of her culinary skills had sounded great at the time, none of the Cesare men had been prepared for her to bake bruschetta among half-naked bodies in South Beach's most racy club.

Giselle garnished the teriyaki dishes with a curly strip of orange peel and a healthy chunk of Tuscan bread while Renzo rang a pager to signal one of the wait staff.

"Admittedly, no. I'm not an expert since men never get close enough to me to break my heart thanks to you." She frowned up at him, her forehead damp with steam from the stove.

"Just because the last guy you dated didn't break your heart doesn't mean he didn't cause you a hell of a lot of grief. Excuse me for trying to make sure that doesn't happen again." Some married SOB had lied to Giselle that he was single and taken her for a ride last winter. Renzo still hadn't forgiven himself for not keeping a better eye out for her.

"I'm entitled to make my own mistakes, damn it. You and Nico have suffocated me with big brother watchfulness ever since then. If you don't hook up with some majorly distracting females soon, I may be forced to strangle the both of you."

"Sorry, sis. Cesare men don't throw their women to the wolves, and this place of yours is crawling with them." He snagged a plate of teriyaki for himself along with an extra slice of bread. "But since you're feeding me tonight, I'll give you a reprieve and you can have the next hour to yourself."

Giselle shoved him toward the door. "I swear you and Nico are only playing watchdog so you can eat for free. Will you at least try to look mildly charming and less like a muscle-bound bouncer while you chow down so maybe some naive woman will steal you away for a few days?"

Renzo reached for a bottle of water before he backed out of the kitchen and into the club. "I'm not interested in the kind of women who want to steal me away. Neanderthals need to do all the stealing."

As the heavy metal door swung shut behind him he heard Giselle call him a chauvinist pig and he smiled. No news there.

Dance music flooded his senses as he melted into the crowd to search for a table. Snippets of conversation around him drowned out his own thoughts, escalating into an unintelligible, continuous rumble of noise and laughter.

Although Renzo made no attempt to look charming while he ate at his table for one in the back of the bar, tempting women approached him twice. Part of him responded to their frank come-ons and slinky attire. It had been six months since Celeste, after all. Old-fashioned values be damned, his sister had been right to suggest he was no monk.

But he had more on his mind than sex—even with the thumping bass of R&B music pulsing through the dance club and the swirl of moody red and blue lights above him. As the clock behind one of the bars struck midnight, Renzo told himself he needed to do a better job keeping the wolves from Giselle's door—a sacred trust passed along to him and his brothers by their father on his deathbed. More importantly, he had to figure out how in the hell to pay for his younger brother's latest bills in law school while the rest of his family built their careers.

Obviously he needed a second job to supplement his carpentry, but—

Holy hell.

Renzo's attention snapped from finances back to the action on the dance floor. The scene that a moment ago had been a mass of rump shaking, thigh flashing and heavy breathing got a little more interesting as a petite blonde dressed like a fairy in a high-school play glided into view.

Renzo had her pegged for the glasses and hair-in-a-bun type in two seconds flat. Her fluttery lavender dress looked like the kind of thing other women wore to church. Yet here she was, flitting through South Beach's most notoriously exotic club in an ankle length skirt.

She had a schoolteacher walk too. Very proper. No lazy hip rolling or swinging of arms going on there. In fact, she seemed to take up as little space as possible, edging her way through the crowd, shoulders delicately drawn in and her blue eyes wide with palpable surprise at the sex-drenched atmosphere.

She stood out in the crowd to him a conservative anomaly in the room packed full of skintight clothes and do-me high heels.

Not that anyone else seemed to notice.

While Renzo tracked her with his eyes as she inched her way between men and women playing complex games of flirtation, he realized no one else noticed the incongruity of this reserved creature in the midst of the urban jungle.

Talk about being thrown to the wolves. The feathery blonde looked completely unprepared to handle herself in a flagrant meat market like this one. Where was *her* big brother, damn it?

Rising to his feet, Renzo passed off his plate to a harried busboy and moved closer to the dance floor, all thought of second jobs and law school tuition forgotten for the moment.

Not that he was attracted to this woman, he told himself. Just that the protector in him couldn't stand to watch her brand of innocence stomped by the lascivious lounge lizards populating the club.

He had already glimpsed some slick Don Juan type headed her way, two drinks in his hand. And no way did this man know the wide-eyed blonde. Renzo had seen this particular Romeo at the club every night he'd checked in on Giselle for the past month. Nico had tossed the guy out on his ear last week for aggressively dancing with a woman who obviously wanted no part of his company.

Renzo finished his bottle of water and tossed it on to the bar, keeping his eye on the silk-suited barracuda closing in on little Miss Innocent. Giselle wouldn't exactly mind if he didn't get back to the kitchen for another hour.

She could call him a chauvinist all she wanted. He had every intention of running interference for the blond newcomer—at least until he convinced her she was out of her depth in these shark-infested waters.

Swearing off women didn't mean he couldn't help out a lady in distress. Or possibly introduce himself after he'd given her a hand. He had a pulse, after all.

And, damn it, he wasn't a monk.

ESMERALDA WONDERED if it was too late to back out of the blind date thing when she spied the man in a slick silk suit walking toward her with two drinks in his hand. He shared the same reedy, too-perfect good looks as her former boss, an association that brought a wave of nausea to her already quivery belly.

She forced herself to stand still, however, determined not to follow her instincts tonight. If this guy turned out to be Hugh Duncan, she would find a way to survive it. Although she suspected it would be easier to get through the evening if she'd worn her bra. At this rate, she'd be hunching her shoulders all night to disguise the fact.

Then again, her date might be very nice despite the strong cloud of musky cologne that reached her long before he did.

Her lovely neighbor Mrs. Wolcott assured her Hugh was a perfect gentleman.

Straightening her spine as the man approached her from the right and opened his mouth to speak, Esme jumped when another voice intervened.

"I've been keeping an eye out for you." The warm, masculine rasp emanated from her left. Somehow she'd missed this man's approach in her fear of turning her back on Mr. Reedy.

A damn shame considering the newcomer looked like a page on a girl's pinup calendar. She had never possessed such a thing herself, but in the many hours of her life she'd spent ensconced in bookstores, Esme had most certainly spied hunk calendars. This guy, with his dark hair, even darker eyes and sexy bronze skin should have been in one of the "Studs of Italy" editions.

Not that she'd memorized her favorite titles or anything, either.

"You've been looking for me?" She wondered if her voice conveyed a pathetic amount of hopefulness. Glancing back and forth between Mr. Reedy who'd taken the liberty of ordering a drink for her already and the Italian stud who possessed killer muscles and yet not a hint of aggressive body language, Esme crossed her fingers that the Italian stud proved to be Hugh Duncan.

She cast a pointed look to her left, away from the overpowering cologne of Joe Slick. "I'm Esme Giles. Are you Hugh?"

The guy to her right bristled, raising himself a little taller in his polished leather shoes as he shoved a drink under her nose. "Hey, Esme, how about some sex on the beach?"

She struggled not to roll her eyes. Even the college history geeks had been above using that tired bit. Curious, she wanted to ask the man if that line had ever worked for him before, but Mr. Tall, Dark and Delicious inserted himself between them to face her.

"*I'm* the man you're looking for." He nudged the reedy guy's glass aside with one hand while smoothly steering Esme toward the back of the club and away from the other man.

Very presumptuous. And okay, maybe a little sexy.

Part of her was grateful for the assistance since she'd been getting a sinus headache from the other guy's cologne overload, but part of her didn't appreciate being led around by the nose. Or in this case, the elbow.

The new Esmerelda had every intention of calling her own shots and following her own path in life.

She stopped just before they reached a secluded table, refusing to go any farther until she'd confronted Rambo.

Whirling on him, she sent her skirt in a swirl about her legs, the resulting breeze creating a delicious draft up her dress. But as she faced her rescuer again, she was struck anew by his sexy good looks. The bronze skin, the dark eyes, the longish dark hair. His sharply sculpted face was full of hard angles, relieved only by the soft fullness of his mouth.

And despite the serious feminine competition all around, this guy had noticed *her* and stuck around long enough to help her out of a sticky situation. The night seemed to be looking up.

Clearing her throat, she tried to remember Mrs. Wolcott's description of Hugh Duncan and failed.

Any mental vision she might have formed of Hugh had somehow transmuted into the hard edges and clean lines of the man standing in front of her. "I'm sorry, but did you say you were my date?"

"You're meeting a blind date?" His dark eyebrows knit together in an intimidating furrow. "In this meat market?"

What a perfectly eloquent assessment of the place. Club Paradise was lushly beautiful with its rich appointments and clever lighting, but the atmosphere in the lounge was a bit—sexually overt. Mrs. Wolcott had given Esme a room here tonight so she would have safe territory to retreat to if her date didn't work out. "It *is* a meat market, isn't it?"

He grumbled something unintelligible under his breath about idiotic men as a group of dancers clad only in strategic white feathers breezed past them.

She noted with interest that his gaze didn't stray to the expanse of exposed feminine flesh that passed almost under his nose. If anything, she had been more curious about the feathered dancers than he seemed.

Appreciation for meeting a real gentleman—something far too rare in her opinion—warmed her to her toes. And he'd known she was meeting a blind date. Obviously she had found her man. "If you think Club Paradise is such a pick-up joint, why did you want to come here tonight?"

"This wouldn't have been my first choice, that's for sure. Who was it you said you were meeting again?"

He glared around the room as if surprised to find himself here.

"Hugh Duncan." She snagged a fresh prepoured glass off the champagne fountain at one end of the bar and helped herself to a little more of the bubbly drink. As part of ladies night, the Moulin Rouge Lounge offered free champagne to its female guests until 1:00 a.m., according to a sign in the lobby. She'd had a glass a few minutes ago, but the nervousness chugging through her and the tingly awareness of the man standing next to her urged her to indulge in a little more. Between the rapid pounding of her heart and the swift whoosh of air in and out of her lungs, the sedative effects of alcohol would be most welcome right about now. "I'm so glad I found you. I have to admit I'm a little out of my element in here. I feel better already to be with someone I can trust."

He was quiet for so long, she hesitated before sipping her champagne.

"Assuming you *are* my date tonight?" A wave of nervousness threaded through her. She'd be a little bit embarrassed at this point if he wasn't.

He reached for the glass just as she put it to her lips, covering her hand with his own, effectively seizing the drink and awakening a long slumberous desire she hadn't known she'd harbored until just this very moment.

"Why don't you let me get you a drink?" He leaned closer as he spoke in soft, serious tones. The gesture was at once totally innocent and thoroughly intimate.

His dark eyes cut through the shifting blue and red lights, making the rest of the noisy club disappear for one heated moment. "And I am most definitely your date tonight, Esme Giles."

2

RENZO EASED the champagne glass out of Esme's hand slowly, not wishing to scare her away by appearing too domineering. Didn't she know the dangers of picking up a prepoured glass of anything in a crowded nightclub?

He'd have to talk to Giselle about getting rid of those filled glasses on top of the champagne fountain right away. The drinks were perched in a place where anyone could have access to them—not a good setup when date-rape drugs were so widespread. It took half a second for someone to drug a drink, a stat savvy club-goers kept in mind.

Not Esme Giles.

Her brand of innocence could be downright dangerous.

Applying light pressure to the small of her back, Renzo nudged her toward the table he'd staked out for himself in the back. Over her head, he crooked his finger at one of Giselle's waitresses.

"Why don't you let me order you a fresh drink?" He rolled out the Cesare charm, needing to keep Esme entertained and out of circulation in the lounge. "My sister is something of a food and drink wizard and she works in the back. How about if I ask her to prepare us something a little more exotic?''

Esme seemed to weigh the idea for a moment. Then she smiled up at him in a half-cocked grin that struck him as a rusty movement. "Yes. Absolutely. Exotic is exactly what I'm looking for tonight."

God help him.

If she'd said as much to Don Juan the barfly who'd tried to corner her before, the guy would have hustled her out of the club and back to his room in five minutes flat.

Apparently Esme had no sense of how to protect herself in the bar scene.

And although Renzo hadn't intended to misrepresent himself tonight, he also wasn't about to allow Esme to wander the club alone looking for her idiotic blind date.

What kind of moron lured an innocent woman like Esme into the most scandal-ridden hot spot in South Beach? A guy who didn't deserve her, that much was for damn sure. For that matter, maybe this Hugh person had sleazy intentions.

In which case, Renzo definitely wasn't going to let him have a shot at her.

As he and Esme slid into the seats of the round booth table in the back corner, Renzo asked the waitress for a couple of Good Fortune Potions, Giselle's most recent creation.

He'd simply enjoy a drink with Esme until he could put her safely in a cab back home. Surely he could justify not telling her the truth since he was only protecting her. It's not like he had designs on her for himself.

Still, in an effort to forestall any questions about him, Renzo thought he'd better take the conversational lead.

"Esme is a great name." Okay, admittedly his dating small-talk skills needed a little sharpening up, but it was the best he could come up with on short notice.

"Short for Esmerelda, but that's a bit of a mouthful." She peered around the club from the safe haven of their table, her dark-blue eyes absorbing the action with the passive interest of a woman accustomed to observing life rather than taking part. "My mother thought if she gave her daughter an exotic name I would eventually live up to it." Esme gave a shrug, her exposed shoulder calling attention to itself a few feet away from him. "But no luck so far. I'm an out-of-work art historian with an interest in antiques. Not exactly the outgoing and adventurous type."

Renzo allowed his gaze to wander over her again with this new information in mind. But his eye was distracted by the shadow of her body beneath her dress and the...

Holy hell.

She was naked underneath that dress.

Thank you, God, he wasn't in the middle of taking a drink or he would have spewed it for sure. Luckily the waitress chose to make a reappearance just then, bringing with her a tray laden with the exotic concoction his sister had demanded he taste just last night for the first time. The blend of fruit juices, rum and who knows what else, garnished by a fortune cookie had been delicious.

Esme reached for hers, a gesture that put her breasts in close contact with the silky thin fabric of her lavender dress. Breasts he could now see that were shaped like small apples, tipped with dark, tight nipples.

A rush of male appreciation swamped his senses, alerting his every stray blood cell that a sexy woman sat within tantalizing reach. Heat crawled over his skin, making his whole body edgy and very...ready for action.

Great. This was just what he needed—he was trying to be noble and in the course of two steamy seconds his body had turned traitor to the cause.

How had he ever thought that dress of hers was conservative?

"I'm sure you're living up to the name." His words scratched across a throat gone slightly hoarse. Maybe this swearing off women thing hadn't been such a good idea. His self-imposed sexual deprivation of the last few months was robbing him of necessary objectivity. "You risked accepting a blind date tonight. That takes a healthy sense of adventure."

"Maybe a little." She sipped her drink through the straw, her forehead puckered in wary concentration as she tasted the concoction. And smiled. "My compliments to your sister. This is delicious. Much better than champagne."

She bent forward for another sip, her breasts grazing the fabric of her dress again. Not that he had a clear view with the table in the way and her sitting at a forty-five degree angle to him in the round booth. Still, his imagination easily supplied what he couldn't see with his own eyes.

"You're an art historian?" Think conversation. Think conversation. He refused to morph into some slick pickup artist just because he'd caught a glimpse of bare breasts. He could maintain an intelligent discussion even if Esme was naked beneath her dress. He hoped.

"I just left a position with the South Beach historical museum that I held for five years. We focused on preserving Floridian culture and we recently added a small exhibit on native architecture." She did a double take as the lights dimmed on the dance floor and the music changed to a salsa beat. The club-goers who had peopled the floor moved to one side to make room for the hourly show. Leaning close, she whispered in Renzo's ear. "What's happening now?"

Warmth tripped through him along with her hushed words. What was it about a whisper that created an immediate veil of intimacy around two people?

"There's a floor show every hour. Sort of a Vegas-style event with lots of—" Half-naked bodies. Painted-on tattoos over women's nipples. See-through feathers in the place of panties. "—costumes."

She'd see for herself soon enough. The parade of

perfect female bodies and fluffy white feathers was already snaking through the club toward the open dance floor. He and Nico had been trying for weeks to convince Giselle that the sex-drenched club was no place for a young woman to work, but to no avail so far.

Renzo didn't take any note of the parade of bare flesh, however. He simply watched Esme's reaction, mesmerized by her transparent features as her face registered surprise, titillation and pleasure at the seductive moves performed by the Moulin Rouge's dancers.

Her cheeks flushed pink the first time a dancer sent a limber high kick in their direction. Her soft lips parted on a little gasp when another woman brought her supple bump-and-grind routine a few inches from their table.

Was Esmerelda Giles—who, according to her, had never quite lived up to her name—as innocent as she appeared? She had to be in her mid-to-late twenties if she'd worked as an art historian for five years. Didn't that sort of profession call for some kind of postgraduate work? Surely she couldn't be all that inexperienced. But there was an undeniable naiveté about her actions, an unexpected sense of wonder Renzo found incredibly appealing.

So many women he'd dated were blatantly in charge of their sexual desire. The dating mentality these days seemed to be I want this, I want it nonstop for 12.2 minutes and I don't want to wait for it. Did it make him a chauvinist to think that in women's rush for control in the bedroom a certain willingness to go with the flow, an openness to try new things, had been lost?

Spontaneity seemed like a quaint notion of the past.

However, it seemed like a quality Esme Giles might possess.

Too bad he wasn't going to act on the growing attraction he felt for her.

Besides, Esme wasn't the sort of woman a guy could just cart back to his room. She was more demure than that. More subtle. A woman with delicate ethics and old-fashioned values.

JUST *HOW* DID A WOMAN go about enticing an Italian stud back to her bedroom?

Esme pondered the question as she stared across the table at her sexy-as-sin date.

The seductive performance of the feather-clad dancers had just ended and the music pulsing through the club switched from the blood-pumping salsa to a funky R&B song that had everyone on the floor. Something about the staged show remained with Esme, some vaguely erotic longing, a latent desire to perform and be noticed in the bold manner the dancers had called attention to themselves.

If she could claim that kind of sensual power, she would surely be an in-charge woman to be reckoned with. A fierce female. A woman who ran with the wolves.

All of which was exactly what she needed. And she'd be on her way to having those things with one simple seduction.

The decision to pursue her date wasn't nearly as difficult as she might have expected. She couldn't deny an instant attraction to his dark good looks and his fathomless brown eyes. Under normal circumstances she would have crossed her fingers that he would call her—knowing all the time he wouldn't—and wasted a lot of time being disappointed.

But under her new life principle, she would do the opposite of wait around. She'd call the shots, she'd seduce him, and maybe—just maybe—she'd actually get what she wanted in life for a change.

Simple.

Of course, Esme fully recognized the brilliant plan was probably helped along by the happy combination of champagne and Good Fortune Potion zipping through her system. Other women did this all the time, however, so she refused to worry about the consequences.

Her date—Hugh, she reminded herself—leaned closer, the short sleeve of his black T-shirt brushing her shoulder as he did. "So what did you think of the show? The Moulin Rouge Lounge has caused a bit of a local uproar with the antics of their dancers."

Esme rejoiced over the conversational opening and prayed she wouldn't blow it. "I thought it was incredibly sexy. Very...stimulating. Definitely inspiring."

Hugh's jaw dropped just a little. Esme hoped that was a good sign.

"Really? Some of our local politicians are making a push to put more restrictions on the creative license of the performance."

"The audience is appropriately mature here." Esme shook her head, thinking of all the risqué artworks from antiquity that were accumulating dust in the basements and storerooms of museums all over the world. "Throughout history, there has always been a movement to suppress sexual art, but who exactly is getting hurt in the wake of a little titillation at an adult dance club?" She cast him what she hoped was a suggestive smile and flipped her hair over one shoulder. "So a few more men and women go home together tonight because a provocative dance has gotten them fired up. What harm is there in that?"

Hugh's dark eyes widened.

Did he have no clue what she was driving at here? Perhaps a woman needed to be more overt about what she wanted.

"I agree there's no harm," he started, the words seeming to stick in his throat a bit.

Esme rushed to clarify. "All I'm saying is that we ought to be able to appreciate the invitation to seduction without feeling guilty because we enjoyed it, you know?"

Hugh shrugged. "I wouldn't say *I* feel guilty. But some people—"

"That's great." She squeezed his forearm, relishing

the way a man's arm contained muscle in the most innocuous of places and hoping positive reinforcement would help steer him in her direction. "Because I don't feel guilty either. You want to walk me up to my room?"

"You have a room here?" His voice rasped across another throaty note.

Esme handed him his half-full goblet. "Tonight was a birthday present from your aunt. Mrs. Wolcott reserved a room for me when she set up our date so I wouldn't have to worry about taking a bus home."

"I would have never put you on a bus at two o'clock in the morning, Esme." His dark eyebrows knit together in that serious manner that warmed her insides. Hugh Duncan knew enough about chivalry to make a woman's heart beat faster.

"Maybe Mrs. Wolcott just wanted to give me a place to retreat to in case our date didn't go as well as she'd hoped." The dear woman. Esme couldn't wait to give her a big hug and some homemade bread for sending this gorgeous man into her life if only for one night.

"About my aunt—"

Esme jumped up from the table, certain that this line of conversation would only distract them from the flirtatious atmosphere she'd struggled to maintain ever since the feathered dancers had departed the lounge.

Doting aunts were not a topic she wished to discuss while in seduction mode for the first time in her life.

"How about one dance before we call it a night?" She extended her hand to him in yet another unprecedented move. Esme Giles, the woman who'd busted the grading curve in every class she'd ever taken, the college geek turned scholar for life, was asking the most gorgeous guy in the room to dance with her.

And as if her lucky stars were in perfect alignment over her head, the DJ changed the pace to a slow groove, a song that was sexy and danceable and just right for getting close to this man.

Either because of his chivalrous nature or else because he knew fate was conspiring against him, Hugh slid out of the booth and rose to his feet. Esme gulped as his arm slipped around her waist, the warm expanse of his palm connecting with the small of her back.

"How can I refuse a beautiful woman's request?"

Oh my.

No one had ever called her beautiful before. Cute, maybe. And she knew better than to fall for idle flattery, but something about the way he looked at her when he said it made her feel beautiful. Strong. Confident.

As they made their way toward the floor, Esme revised her former opinion that she had been overdressed for tonight. Right now, with long masculine fingers applying light pressure to her spine, she felt as if she wore nothing at all. The thin silk of her dress seemed to scorch and vanish beneath that sure, possessive touch.

She scoped out the dance floor, hoping to find a place for them among the mob of other couples vying for space on the hardwood floor. But she needn't have concerned herself. Before she'd analyzed all the options, Hugh twirled her toward him, somehow halting her midspin so that she ended up face to face with him, firmly in his arms.

Every schoolgirl fantasy she'd ever hoped for in vain was granted in that long minute as she stared up at him. It didn't matter that she'd never been greatly noticed, fawned over or otherwise admired by a charismatic male in the course of her younger days because right now the forces of cosmic balance were finally tipping the scale in her favor.

And she was winning big.

She could have gazed into those dark brown eyes of his forever, but the subtle sway of their feet beneath them jolted her back to awareness. They were dancing.

Not the awkward one-two-three, one-two-three of stepping on one another's feet that had been a staple in her personal repertoire. No, she wasn't even sure *how* they were dancing or *why* her body knew just how to follow his, but they moved together in supple agreement as smoothly as if they'd been choreographed.

His body met hers—hip to hip, thigh to thigh—in a warm, sinuous connection. Her skin flamed right through her silken skirt as she realized how little a barrier her gypsy dress provided. And her breasts...

She didn't dare move away from him now that her

breasts grazed his chest. Her reaction—and attraction—would be immediately obvious.

The music enveloped them, folding her into the slow bass line as the dance floor lights all turned to a moody shade of blue. In the dimness, she could almost convince herself they were alone as they moved together in total accord.

"Thanks for sharing a drink with me tonight, Esme." His voice emanated from above her, but she was close enough to hear the rumble of speech in his chest. Through the thin layer of black cotton that covered superb pecs. Through the faded pine scent of his aftershave that she only detected now that he was near.

"I hope your aunt didn't have to twist your arm into coming tonight." She kicked herself as soon as she said it because it sounded like the kind of paranoid comment an eighteen-year-old would make. Did she not only have to monitor all her actions but her speech now, too?

He didn't look turned off by her insecure comment, however. He trailed a thumb over her cheek and tipped her face up to his.

"No one twisted my arm, Esme. You were a definite choice of my free will."

Something inside her sighed with pleasure.

Gooseflesh popped out over her skin, a mix of shivery chills and tingly anticipation. His sure touch made her eyelids flutter, fall closed for one long moment.

When the kiss that she'd hoped for didn't materialize, she pried her lids open again and decided the *new* Esme wasn't a woman willing to wait. The new Esme wanted her kiss, by God, and she was determined to have it.

Now.

Confident that her bold decision fit in with her plan to take charge of her life, she pressed her body closer to his.

She hadn't been prepared for the shock waves that kind of movement would send straight to the intimate heart of her. She was in way over her head with this man, but she found she didn't care.

More than anything, she wanted this one chance to be daring, this one night to be bold and in control of her body, her actions.

He readjusted his hands to accommodate their new closeness, his hands on her waist while his fingertips dangled pleasantly down the curve of her backside. Esme wondered what it might be like to make love to him, to have him lower his hands even more to guide their bodies together...

Smoothing her hands up the hard planes of his chest, she inched her way closer to what she wanted. He stared down at her with steady dark eyes, fully alert to her every move yet letting her choose the pace of what was happening between them.

After those horrifying moments locked in her creepy former boss's office, Esme appreciated Hugh's willingness to let her take the lead.

And damn it, she *was* taking the lead.

Even though her senses were all keenly tuned to the moment, a small part of her rational brain stood aloof from the heated action on the dance floor and seemed to stare down at her from above, applauding her boldness.

You go, girl.

As the final strains of the slow song hummed through her, Esme reached for the prize she'd been dreaming of since she laid eyes on her sexy blind date. And with no more thought of the consequences, she touched her lips to his.

3

RENZO CESARE HAD kissed plenty of women in his day.

Not that he considered himself a connoisseur or anything, because that just sounded plain sleazy. But he had some experience to compare Esme Giles's kiss against, and that tentative brush of her soft pink mouth over his completely obliterated all memory of holding anyone else in his arms.

He'd told himself he would let her set the pace tonight since he'd intercepted her from meeting her real date in the first place. According to his sister, no woman wanted to be insulated from life by a hulking Cesare male who would claim mob affiliation in a heartbeat if it would scare potential predators.

Yet here he was, doing his gentlemanly best to save Esme Giles from herself and all the while falling under the spell of her sweet pink lips.

Lips he found himself parting with the sweep of his tongue. Damn. Damn. Damn. He hadn't meant to do that.

But man, she was sweet.

She tasted like rum and something more sugary. Sort of like the strawberry lip gloss girls in his junior high used to wear. All innocence. How had he gone his whole adult life without realizing strawberry lip gloss still turned him on nearly twenty years later?

Her body sank into his a little more, giving him all the more appreciation for the shape and feel of her bare breasts beneath her dress.

Goodbye all innocence. Hello sensual woman.

The hard beads of her nipples had his body answering hers in kind, encouraging him to do all the things to her they both wanted so badly....

Except they were in the middle of a goddamn dance floor.

Renzo broke their kiss, unable to pull away from her totally without disrupting her balance. Besides, he didn't dare move away from her quickly or he'd end up exposing them both a bit too...intimately.

Esme's eyes remained closed a moment, and when she lifted her lids to gaze up at him again, the passion-clouded expression he saw there made him want to drag her somewhere private and—

Wait.

Wasn't he supposedly saving her from that kind of fate when he'd told her a whopper of a fib tonight?

Backing them off the side of the floor, Renzo peeled himself away from her with more than a little regret.

"Maybe you ought to walk me up to my room now," she whispered, her voice barely audible above the synthesized whine of the next dance song.

"Good idea." Renzo steered her through the crowd,

using his body as a shield for her to make sure no drunken idiots copped a feel on the way.

He could not, should not, would not, get any more involved with Esme. The whole charade had been ill-conceived and it would be least embarrassing for all parties concerned if he simply said good-night to her right now.

Just as soon as he knew she was safely inside her room.

Once they cleared the Moulin Rouge Lounge and hit the bank of elevators, she paused, fishing in her purse.

"I'm on the fourth floor in the Sensualist's Suite. Maybe I'd better find my key." She shook her purse as the elevator arrived. Apparently convinced the key lay within the white satin bag, Esme began the search with determination etched on her delicate jawline.

"The Sensualist's Suite?" He had no idea why he tortured himself by asking as they stepped inside the elevator.

Maybe because liars deserved to be tortured.

Withdrawing the plastic card from her bag as they soared up to the necessary floor, Esme's cheeks flushed lightly. "It's the kind of room that has to be seen to be believed. I had no idea the accommodations here were so..." Her eyes darted about the tiny elevator cabin—outfitted in soft brown suede walls and decorated with a fake-leopard-print-covered bench—as if in search for the right word. Finally, her gaze landed on him. "...so sexy."

His body twitched in reaction to the word rolling off her tongue. In reaction to their proximity in the quiet privacy of the small space.

The torture had officially begun.

"My sister told me all the rooms were redesigned when the hotel went from a couples resort to more of a singles haven." As the doors slid open on the fourth floor, Renzo's hand moved automatically toward her waist to help her out of the elevator.

Just before his fingers made contact with the small of her back, he caught himself. If he touched her once, he might never stop. At the last moment, he redirected his errant hand toward the open doors button and pressed that instead.

"Hotels are always remodeling," Esme remarked as she strode down the hall, her gait more confident and easy now that they were alone. Maybe she just didn't enjoy crowds. "This is different. This is spectacular."

Too late, Renzo realized they had arrived at her door and that she was already unlocking it. Opening it.

And somehow they were in the middle of a conversation about her room, which she now wanted to show him.

His feet paused at the threshold of the door—his brain knowing he probably shouldn't enter, the rest of him already straining to follow her.

Esme watched him expectantly as she held the door open with her slight form, her blue eyes communicating silent invitation.

Maybe as long as he kept his distance, maintained an arm's length between them at all times, he could at least check out the room and make sure this Hugh character wasn't lurking in the closet or anything. His aunt had paid for the room, after all. What if the guy thought he was entitled to help himself?

Convinced he *needed* to go inside for just a minute, Renzo whispered a swift prayer for restraint and followed her into the suite.

FOR A MOMENT, Esme had feared she might have to break out a crane to transport the man into her suite. Was it *that* big a decision to come home with her for the night?

Feminine pride stinging just a little, Esme realized she would never be cut out for the club-hopping and manhunting that other South Beach women engaged in with ease. She liked getting to know people before she invited them back to her hotel room.

For that matter, there would be real safety issues at stake here tonight if her date hadn't been given the thumbs-up by her friend and neighbor. At least Esme could feel comfortable knowing Hugh Duncan wasn't a wanted criminal or anything.

His low whistle of appreciation jolted Esme back to the moment. A whistle intended for the exotic room decor and not her, she realized with dismay as his dark eyes swept the width of the suite and the rainbow of earth tones someone had thoughtfully woven into all the furnishings.

Touchable silk and damask pillows littered the dark mahogany furniture while a huge swath of embroidered taupe linen lined the ceiling with a tentlike effect. And if the decadent tent weren't impressive enough, the Sensualist's Suite also boasted a small brook winding through the room.

At least the beautifully appointed room was a comfortable topic. She could spend a little while distracting him with small talk that genuinely interested her before she ambushed him with another kiss.

Assuming she didn't lose her nerve.

Judging by how long it took him to make that final step into her hotel room, Esme guessed he would walk away if she kissed him too soon. For some reason, fate had laughed at her attempts to be bold and brazen tonight by handing her a date with values as traditional as hers had always been.

Just her luck.

"It's gorgeous, isn't it?" Having no idea how to behave while seducing a man, Esme scoured her brain for role models.

Her mother had raised her alone, content to make Esme the center of her world when Esme's father had walked out on his pregnant girlfriend. And Esme's deep love of antiques and art had absorbed her for so many years she barely kept up friendships enough to know how any of her casual acquaintances would go about picking up a man.

The seductive women in the Pre-Raphaelite paintings she loved were often reclining objects to be adored, not active seductresses themselves. No help in that quarter either. The lone source of inspiration she came up with were her screen idols. And if her matinee memory served, Esme thought Bette Davis would have already been mixing the drinks by now.

She hurried to the wet bar and eyed the myriad of offerings in the room service cooler. Too bad they didn't prepackage Good Fortune Potion. She could use a healthy serving right about now—the good luck as much as the potion.

Emerging from the cooler with a miniature bottle of brandy and two snifters—wouldn't Bette be proud?—Esme found Hugh stooping to dip his fingers in the narrow waterfall that trickled gently from one wall in the living area.

"The details are genius." He picked up a smooth river stone from the base of the waterfall where a cleverly crafted brook wound its way through the room. "I've seen something like this in Caribbean resorts before, but the finishes are usually more obviously prefabricated. The polished rocks are a nice touch."

Esme flicked on the stereo located under the bar. She had no clue where the speakers were actually located, but the strains of Brahms seemed to surround them. She hoped classical music wasn't off-putting, but it would be too much of a lie for her to flick over to some hip-hop station and pretend to be a happening chick.

Besides, how could anyone not love Brahms? The

music hadn't been around for centuries because it was no good.

"The furniture is what gets me. Whoever designed the room didn't just pick up the furnishings at the local discount warehouse." With a little awkward fumbling but no major spills, Esme managed to remove the packaging around the top of the brandy bottle and pour two glasses.

Hugh released the pebble he'd been holding and shook the water off his fingertips as he moved toward a small table where she'd set her keys. "Neoclassical reproductions. Nice stuff."

Esme nearly dropped the brandy snifters as she stumbled over her feet. How had he known that? "That's quite an eye you have. A lot of people wouldn't know an antique if they lived with one, let alone be able to name the period."

"But we both know an up-and-coming South Beach singles resort wouldn't exactly have the funds to decorate their rooms with French Empire period mahogany, so I don't think guessing this is a reproduction was much of a stretch." He lifted the small table off the floor and peered underneath the silk panel inset that decorated its surface. "It's not signed but it ought to be. Good replicas are hard to find."

She promptly lost her heart to the man who spoke her language. As he set the table down, she handed him his glass. "You're interested in antiques?" Did it make her a total geek that her heart pounded harder at the thought? "Because I deal in them as a sideline to my museum job. Well, my former job. I used to funnel a lot of antique finds to clients of the museum."

She'd been an art historian by trade for the last five years, but her hobby had always been antiques. Every weekend of her adult life had been devoted to haunting local flea markets and garage sales in an endless quest for precious finds.

"I guess I've learned a few things about antiques through woodworking. I do some carpentry." He tossed back a gulp of his brandy and pointed to the ceiling draped with embroidered linen as if eager to focus the conversation away from himself. "The tent effect is cool."

"And very in keeping with the sensualist's theme." After sniffing the brandy, Esme couldn't bring herself to actually try it. Ack. Maybe she would become equally intoxicated by inhaling the fumes. "Everything in the room just makes you want to reach out and touch, doesn't it?"

Hugh's gaze snapped to hers as if he suspected her words for the blatant come-on that they were meant to be.

But damn it, he seemed to willfully ignore all her subtleties. Almost as though he'd backed off getting any closer to her since they had kissed.

Yet she knew the kiss had been good. Better than good, in fact. Her body still sang with the want of him.

"The fabrics are all top-of-the-line," he agreed, wandering farther away to admire the babbling brook tripping through the room again. He put more distance between them at the same time he put himself closer to the door.

And didn't that say a lot about her charms?

Then again, she had read somewhere in a magazine that in this era of political correctness, men were more careful not to proceed physically with a new woman unless the female was very clear that was what she wanted. So maybe Hugh was simply being upstanding and polite.

But take-charge Esme didn't need her date to be so solicitous. She needed him to kiss her again in the way that tripped off a reverberating alleluia chorus in her brain.

Time to set the record straight.

Resting her brandy on the little table—sorry, Bette—Esme struggled to connect with her inner wild woman as she closed the distance between her and Hugh.

Her instincts told her to try and entice him into kissing her again. So of course, she needed to ignore that instinct and move straight to kissing him herself.

Consequences be damned.

"When I said everything in the room makes you want to reach out and touch, I wasn't just referring to the fabrics." Her pulse jackhammered against her wrist, her neck, her chest. Her words seemed to hover in the heated current of air between them, wrapping them in a suggestive cocoon Hugh couldn't possibly escape.

"You weren't?" He set his drink down now, too, providing her with his complete, undivided attention.

Either that, or he was freeing up his hands so he could sprint away if she got any closer.

"No, I wasn't." She took a measured half step nearer to him, watching him carefully to see if he would flee.

He remained rooted to the spot, his dark eyes raking over her with a heat that didn't feel so polite any more.

"I was referring to a different kind of touching altogether." She edged closer until she could rest her fingertips on the black cotton expanse of T-shirt stretching over his chest.

Hard muscle rippled underneath her touch. His breath hissed out between his teeth. "You're a woman full of surprises, Esme Giles, but I don't know if—"

Stretching up on her toes, she kissed him into silence.

Maybe he had been about to voice a valid concern, but she wasn't in the mood to hear it. If he wanted out of this moment and this kiss, he was going to have to find his own way *not* to be subtle.

But from where she was standing, he didn't strike her as a man who wanted out of the kiss. His arms banded around her with a strength that made her shiver. And this time, she didn't wait for him to stroke his tongue over her lips and seek entry. She parted her lips on contact, ready to receive more of him.

A low groan rumbled through his chest. She didn't

hear it so much as feel it, almost as if he'd stifled the sound. Still, she knew the sentiment had been there.

He wanted this as much as she did and the knowledge fired her with more resolve to wear down his defenses and show him exactly what she wanted tonight.

She'd never minded her lack of a love life—well, not too much anyway—when she'd had her work to be passionate about. But now that she'd had that taken away, too, Esme couldn't help but feel a little desperate to be passionate about something.

Hugh Duncan filled the bill oh-so-nicely.

The man was passion personified with his romantic dark eyes, his polite consideration mingled with his scorching kisses. Yes, he definitely lit her fire—and he did so far more thoroughly than any new acquisition to the Floridian architecture exhibit ever had.

Wrapping her arms around his neck, Esme lost herself in the sensations swirling through her. She closed her eyes to the warm earth tones of the suite and focused on the heat they generated together.

The bristly skin of his jaw scraped along her chin, providing a surprising contrast with the soft fullness of his lips. He tasted faintly of brandy and Esme found herself swaying on her feet as she grew all the more intoxicated.

His hands shifted on her back, his fingers smoothing their way over the thin silk of her dress to graze the bare skin of her shoulders exposed by the generous neckline.

She wanted nothing so much as to wriggle her way

out of that dress and feel his hands all over her body, to let the fire he ignited overtake her and burn away any bad memories she harbored of the last time another man had touched her.

Clinging to him with a fierceness that surprised her, Esme backed them deeper into the room, closer to the piece of furniture she wanted to test with him tonight.

The mahogany replica bed that this man recognized as French Empire neoclassical. Dear God, he was a dream come true.

Esme plastered herself to him with abandon, shedding her old reserve with relish. She was in charge here. She could decide what happened tonight.

And she wanted. Oh, how she wanted.

Her hands strayed over his body, absorbing the hard masculine angles of his shoulders and chest, the narrowed hips that housed the most male part of all.

Not ready to go there quite yet, she contented herself to feeling that particular part of him against her belly as she kissed him with all she was worth and continued her relentless track backward to the bed.

Hugh's hands raked through her hair, disturbing carefully arranged curls and making her feel totally decadent, wild, free.

Everything she felt tonight seemed new and different; unlike anything she'd ever experienced before. Sex in her experience had always been a secret, covert act committed in the dark, not a blazing firestorm that bowled her over before she was even horizontal.

Chills radiated down her spine as his fingers massaged their way through her hair to her scalp and the sensitive back of her neck. Her breasts pressed more urgently against his chest, craving the same attentive touch.

As the back of her leg finally grazed the bed she'd been searching for, Esme was more than ready to topple them on to it. She caved into the taupe-colored duvet, dragging him along with her so that they never broke their kiss.

He landed on top of her with a soft thud, his hands breaking their fall as she knew they would. Something about his very nature, some old-fashioned sense of nobility suggested he would go to great lengths to protect her, to take care of her.

Tucked beneath him, she felt utterly safe and yet deliciously vulnerable at the same time.

Easily shouldering her way out of her dress, she bared her breasts to brush across his chest. Hunger for him curled through her, bold and brazen and demanding to be fed.

He groaned above her, as if her attempt to get naked had tortured him on some sexual level. Esme prayed it was torture in a good way as her body seemed to undulate beneath his on pure sexual instinct.

"Oh my, it's so good," she murmured between kisses as her hand ran down the length of his body to seek the rest of him that she hadn't yet explored. All of him was steely and hard, edgy and muscular. She wanted to explore every inch. "I need you, Hugh."

4

HUGH?

Esme's impassioned cry for another man should have killed the mood and brought Renzo to his senses. But she was responding to his touch, his kiss, his body pressed against hers.

She wanted *him*, not some moron named Hugh who'd trapped her into a blind date at the biggest meat market on the strip. He knew he ought to correct his mistake and confess his ruse before it was too late. And he would.

Just as soon as he stole one peek at the deliciously bare breasts Esme had exposed when she shrugged her way out of her silky dress.

He pulled back to stare down at her and promptly lost track of all his good intentions.

Warm light flickered from the elaborate brass candelabras stationed above the bed in the Sensualist's Suite, casting Esme in a golden glow. Her bare skin bathed in the rosy light, her nipples took on a deep pink tint, the same color as her beckoning lips.

He had no choice but to bend his head to her breast for a taste, a kiss, a decadent feast.

She arched and sighed beneath him, her hands raking through his hair as he fed upon her. Her skin tasted cool and creamy at first, but the longer he allowed his tongue to play over the sweet crests of her nipples, the hotter her flesh became.

Fascinated by her quick response, he lost track of his own, squelching his needs in a desire to please her, to make her cry out. Not until his hands strayed lower to the delicate dip of her belly and the silky curve of her hip beneath the remnants of her dress did he realize that he was teetering on the point of no return himself.

His fingers flexed into her gentle curves as he willed them into obedience. He couldn't, shouldn't take this any further.

Would. Not.

"Hugh?" Esme gazed up at him with passion-clouded blue eyes, her hands quick to move over his and nudge his fingers lower. "Please."

He allowed himself a scant second to absorb the feel of her skin, to appreciate the heady drug of having a woman lead him to the exact places he wanted to go.

His fingers grazed a soft band of cotton low on her hip beneath Esme's fallen dress. He could envision the shape and cut of the bikini panties in his hand.

But damn it, he didn't deserve to see them.

Not tonight.

He pulled away, rolling to one side before he forgot he was raised to have some manners. Some freaking self-control.

"I can't." He hated the sound of those words. Hated

that he hadn't cleared up his mistruth before they'd tumbled into Esme's bed tonight.

"You can't?" Esme twisted around to prop herself on her shoulder. "You mean you're not properly equipped? Because, believe it or not, they sell the necessary..." She drew a circle in the air with one finger, almost as if winding herself up to locate the words she sought. "...protective devices in the snack dispenser under the minibar."

She peered across the beige satin pillows at him with such earnest practicality and only slightly banked passion that Renzo knew without a doubt he was the biggest heel in Miami tonight. This incredible woman would have trusted him with her body if he'd just been honest from the start.

Now, she would no doubt kick him to the curb. But worse, she just might be hurt by his actions and the thought presented him with the promise of a far more stinging pain than being booted out the door.

"It's not that." He laid a hand on her bare shoulder, consumed with the need to touch her once more before those trusting eyes turned shuttered. Angry. "I haven't been totally honest with you, Esme, and I need to straighten out a misunderstanding before we take this any further."

"What do you mean?" She stiffened. He could feel her body go rigid underneath his palm. She reached for the top of her fallen dress, pulling the lavender silk over her breasts and dislodging his hand at the same time.

His fingers mourned the loss of her soft skin, her delicate curves. He braced himself for censure and then unveiled his mistake.

"I'm not really your date. I'm not this Hugh guy you were looking for. My name is Renzo Cesare."

The disillusionment in her eyes provided all the up-braiding he deserved. She didn't need to say how devastating she found this revelation because her transparent features conveyed her horror so eloquently.

And if Renzo had ever thought himself a gentleman, Esme's expression quickly proved him wrong.

For a guy with old-world values who considered himself a protector of women, he'd somehow just betrayed everything he held important.

RENZO?

Esme blinked past the shock, the rip-roaring hurt and embarrassment to get a better handle on exactly what this...*imposter* seemed to be telling her.

"You pretended to be my date?" Maybe the real Hugh Duncan had taken one look at her and fled. Maybe he'd strong-armed a good friend into standing in for him so he wouldn't have to proceed with a blind date from hell tonight. "Why? Did Hugh get cold feet?"

The stranger in her bed had the gall to shrug. *Shrug!* "I don't know. I—I'm not really sure what happened to your date. I just didn't think he could be a very smart guy if he'd asked a woman he never met before to meet him at a place like the Moulin Rouge Lounge. By herself."

He sounded genuinely annoyed about this. As if he had a right to judge the actions of her date. Or her.

Anger bubbled inside her, as strong and fierce as the red-hot desire that had been pulsing through her veins moments ago. Old Esme might have slunk away from this encounter, but new Esme practically sprinted to engage the beast in her bed.

"And you took it upon yourself to judge my decision-making abilities? Why?" Her voice maintained an admirable amount of cool distance despite the knot of embarrassed disappointment that curled in her belly. She couldn't decide if she was more upset at the notion of this man's deception—or at the loss of the fiery interlude that had been almost in her grasp.

God, her luck sucked this month.

Renzo curled to a sitting position, his abs flexing underneath the dark T-shirt she'd been moments away from removing. "I don't know why. I just saw you in the middle of that pickup jungle down there and I knew you didn't belong with all those club-hopping vampires who wait for fresh blood to walk through the door."

"So you decided to be the first vampire in line?" She scrambled to the other side of the bed and straightened her dress back into position. Her unbound hair still grazed the bare patches of her neck and shoulders in a teasing caress, reminding her of the care she'd taken to look her best for this date.

A date she'd never actually met.

"Hell no." His dark eyebrows knit together in a forbidding slash and he had the nerve to sound insulted. "I just couldn't stand to see you harassed by one of those guys while you waited for some loser blind date who didn't know enough to take you someplace nice."

She tried really hard to follow that logic and failed. "What makes you think my date would have been such a loser anyway? And who are you to think you can intercede where you have no damn business?"

"You're right. I had no business to interfere. It's an arrogance thing that goes way back and I don't know why I think I know what's best for people, but damn it, sometimes I do." Hauling himself off the bed, he moved to pace the floor between the bed and the narrow babbling brook. "Don't you know you're never supposed to pick up a prepoured drink at a nightclub, Esme? There are predators out there who will pour date-rape drugs in an unguarded drink faster than you can bat those long eyelashes of yours. You could wake up the next day with no memory of what happened to you or who you went home with." He jammed a hand through his dark hair, pulling the strands back off his angular face. The gesture helped her to fully appreciate the depth of his glare.

"I've read about that," she admitted, realizing he did have a point about that, at least. She would have to be more careful if she ever ventured out on her own to the club scene again.

But after tonight's fiasco, she honestly couldn't see that happening anytime soon.

Plagued with a sudden wave of weariness, Esme's anger eased, leaving her too defenseless to face the pacing Stud of Italy who still dominated her suite.

"I'll talk to my sister about the problem with the champagne bar on ladies' night since she's in charge of the kitchens. As for why I thought your date was a loser…" Renzo halted at the foot of the bed. "I guess I don't have any real grounds for that assumption other than the fact that he asked you to meet him here. I saw you, I wanted you and I told myself he didn't deserve you."

She blinked back at him, not sure she could trust anything he said at this point. The part about him wanting her sent a shiver up her spine, but was that simply a scheming man's fastest route back to bed?

Esme had to admit she'd drifted out of her depth tonight. She couldn't come close to understanding why a man so obviously capable of finding plenty of dates on his own would have intercepted her before she could indulge in her first adventure in years.

Not to mention, her plan to take charge of her life had been a total bust. Bad decision number five thousand thirty-nine—going to bed with the wrong man— had really thrown a wrench in her plans.

"Renzo Cesare, you say?" There wasn't much to do now but send this sexy man away. No matter what he said about saving her from herself and her bad judgment, Esme didn't know what to make of his actions tonight. She couldn't help but think she'd been the butt of some elaborate joke. Rising, she crossed the suite with efficient steps and paused in front of the door with what she hoped was a small measure of dignity. "I wish we could have met under different circumstances. But now that you've walked me safely to my room, I think it's probably time for you to go."

She took great comfort in the coolness of her tone, the resolve in her voice. She tried not to notice the wave of regret she experienced at the thought of what might have been if tonight had been real. Special.

Something about the stubborn set of his square jaw made Esme worry he wouldn't be easily moved. He lingered at the foot of the bed for a long moment before he finally nodded.

"That's wise." He strode across the floor, his long, denim-encased legs covering the terrain quickly despite his lazy pace. "You don't know me from Adam, so it only makes sense to kick me out. You think there's any chance I can redeem myself down the road? Tomorrow? Next week?"

"I don't think that's a good idea." Much as she might be salivating over the play of muscles beneath his T-shirt, she had no interest in playing games when it came to dating. "Besides, I did agree to meet someone here tonight and now I need to find out what happened to him. Maybe reschedule."

Although she had to admit that after kissing Renzo, she wasn't really looking forward to a blind date with anyone else. He might have pulled a fast one on her tonight, but there was no point denying he kissed like a god.

Renzo scowled. "You're not going back downstairs tonight, I hope."

She scowled back just to give him a taste of his own medicine. "Not that it's any of your business, but no, I'm not. I'll try calling Hugh to at least let him know why I didn't show."

Or at least she'd call his aunt and let her know what happened. Renzo didn't need to know she'd never so much as spoken to Hugh Duncan.

"Good. I'll be in the kitchens helping my sister if you need me. I'll be here for at least a couple more hours."

She opened the door, unwilling to participate in any discussion about how much she might need him. She refused to be attracted to a guy who'd lied to her. Stepping back, she stood out of the way to clear a path for him. "Thanks. But I'll be fine."

"I'm sorry about—" Renzo lingered in the doorway "—all of this. I don't know what I was thinking, but I didn't mean to upset you."

Upset? Who was upset?

Just because her Cinderella night was over and her experiment in being bold with her prince had back-fired in the most humiliating way possible? Just because she'd really liked this man she thought was her date?

She wouldn't even go there.

"Good night, Renzo." Esme closed the door behind

him, unconcerned if the heavy weight of it sped him across the threshold all the faster.

She needed to be alone to wade through the mess she'd made of her night. So much for her bid to take charge of her life.

Starting tomorrow, she would pour all of her energies into carving out a new career path and developing her professional goals. She'd always been better with artwork than people.

So what if her dreams would be filled with visions of what might have happened with sexy Renzo Cesare? Her antique watch had long ago struck midnight and she'd obviously lost her glass slipper somewhere between the babbling brook and the minibar. Her luck hadn't been changing for the better. She'd merely earned her most crowning humiliation of all.

The real Prince Charming hadn't even bothered to show up. He'd sent one of the Studs of Italy to take his place and give her tattered pride one final trounce.

THE DOOR CLOSED behind Renzo with echoing finality. Esme couldn't have made it much plainer that she wanted him the hell out of her lush Sensualist's Suite. Still, he had to bite his tongue not to call back through the barrier to remind her to lock up. Did the woman never consider her own safety?

Finally, the dead bolt snicked into place, freeing him from any notion that he was sticking around long enough to be sure she was secure in her room. No, if he continued to linger outside her door now, then he was just the average pathetic guy who got dumped.

Damn.

Except for his misguided trip down the aisle, Renzo had never really been dumped before. Of course, Celeste leaving him at the altar had been a pretty big breakup, but until now, it had been the only time a woman had ever walked away from him.

And hell, even Celeste hadn't left in the middle of foreplay. Esmerelda Giles had to have some major fortitude to break things off when they'd been sending sparks flying all over that fancy suite of hers.

Then again, maybe he overestimated his appeal and it hadn't been that difficult for her to boot him out at all. Now she was calling her *real* date. And even if she had no intention of rescheduling, the realization still stung.

And wasn't that a hell of a note to end the night on?

He strode through the hotel corridor to the elevator, ignoring the pang of regret at the way things had finished between him and Esme. What did he expect when he'd started out a relationship with a lie? At the time he'd misled her into thinking he was her date, however, he hadn't been thinking along those lines. He'd simply meant to make sure the club shark who'd been hitting on her didn't take a bite.

But then they'd started talking and he'd glimpsed a lot more to Esme than just a naiveté about nightlife. She had impressed him with her work as an art historian, then she'd caught him off-guard with the subtle invitations to dance, to walk her back to her room. He'd been too intrigued to set the record straight and too distracted to think through the consequences.

The elevator doors slid open on the lobby level where Renzo stepped out into a small throng of hotel guests and late-night party-goers headed for the nightclub. He followed a long hallway toward the Moulin Rouge Lounge, keeping an eye out for his brother Nico so they could figure out the family finances.

"Hey you dawg." His brother's voice sounded from a darkened nook off the hallway. "Wait up."

Renzo turned in time to catch sight of his brother in a corner near the doors to the stairwell. Nico, a former hockey goon who'd recently swapped his work as an NHL star to a goalie coach for the Miami hockey team, made a hell of an incongruous picture as he gently pried his six-foot-three frame out of a determined redhead's fierce grasp.

When he finally freed himself, Nico fell into step beside Renzo, their feet headed toward the kitchen in silent, mutual agreement. Their sister Giselle ruled the Club Paradise kitchens as the property's executive chef and she could always be persuaded to provide a little late-night sustenance before she closed up shop.

"Who you calling dawg?" Renzo elbowed his brother in the gut. "I'm not the one making time with strangers in every shadowed corner."

Nico smiled at a group of women engaged in lipstick application and hair primping in the hallway near the club doors. It never failed to amaze Renzo that even with a nose broken three times over, his brother could attract hordes of women without really trying. What the hell was there about a zigzag nose that turned women on?

"Oh please. I saw the direction you were walking just now." Nico gave his brother an assessing look. "Don't even pretend like you weren't returning from some hotel room or another."

Busted.

"I just needed to walk a friend to her room. No big deal." Since he'd never been able to lie to his brother without Nico seeing right through him, Renzo tried to stick as close to the truth as possible.

They wound their way through the decadent hotel past a series of framed prints depicting advertisements for old-time peep shows.

"Since when are the hallways of a five-star property unsafe for women to navigate alone? Please, Ren. You're talking to your brother here."

"God forbid a guy act like a gentleman just for the hell of it. Did it ever occur to you that walking someone to her room can be a common courtesy without having carnal implications? No, that's right. NHL players are too busy body-checking anything in their way to concern themselves with something as mundane as courtesy."

They reached the entrance to the main kitchen then or Nico would have surely continued to harass him.

And damn it, Renzo didn't want to think about how badly he'd screwed things up with Esmerelda.

He didn't want to think about her now, but her guileless blue eyes and seriously hot kisses wouldn't leave him alone.

"Enough said, little brother. From all that hissing and snarling you're doing over there, it's painfully apparent you didn't just get laid. No need to try and convince me." Nico ducked out of the way of a waiter balancing a tray on each shoulder and sidled up to a pretty blond waitress filling saltshakers to prep for the next day.

Renzo stormed over to the mammoth-size industrial refrigerator in the kitchen outfitted in top-to-bottom stainless steel.

"Welcome back," his sister called, doling out a few plates of seafood nachos to a server sporting a neck full of tattoos. Giselle sent the waiter on his way and sauntered closer to the fridge. "Dare I hope you met someone tonight since you've been gone for the last four hours?"

"He won't admit anything," Nico supplied from his station beside the blond saltshaker filler. "But judging by his mood, I'd say he didn't get lucky."

Renzo cursed as he stared into the refrigerator and snagged a pink pastry box that was bound to be full of something great. Couldn't his family have any shred of discretion?

No wonder he'd been attracted to Esme. He

couldn't picture her ever blurting out someone else's business the way every member of his family did.

Armed with the pastry box, he shut the fridge and glared at Nico before answering Giselle. "I saw a woman floundering with one of the lounge losers who was coming on a little too strong."

"You're a very effective chaperone, I'll grant you that." Giselle started to smile until her gaze fell on the pastry box. "Wait, Renzo. You can't have those. I baked them for—"

He really didn't want to aggravate his sister, but after missing out on his chance with Esme because he was so damn sure he knew best, he felt utterly deserving of whatever confection rested in the pastry box.

"I only want one." He turned, protecting the box with his body as she reached to wrest it away from him. "Just one, I swear."

He opened the lid as she slugged him on the shoulder.

"You can't, they're—" Her voice died as he got a look at the treats inside.

Pornographic pastries?

"Holy hell!" Renzo gazed down at the two delicious rows of cream puffs frosted in such a way that the delicacies looked exactly like naked breasts. And damned if they didn't look like Esme's breasts—complete with bright-red cherry nipples. "Where did these come from?"

Nico scrambled his way across the kitchen with a speed surprising even for an NHL skater. He reached for one of the adult-only treats but Giselle slapped his hand away.

She yanked the box from Renzo, her cheeks pink with anger or embarrassment, he couldn't be sure. "They came from hours of my hard work and they are selling like hotcakes as specialty items so you can just feed your endless appetite with something less time-intensive, okay?"

"You're trafficking in porno baked goods now?" Nico yelled across the kitchen as Giselle tucked the pink cardboard container back into the refrigerator. He shoved Renzo just enough to get his attention. "You shouldn't have left her for the last four hours, Ren. Bad enough she's working in the most sexually explicit club on the strip, but now she's selling bare breasts on the open market? Pop would have our asses if he knew."

Sensing a familiar Cesare family explosion on the horizon, Renzo nudged his brother toward the door. "It's not like they're real, bro." He tried to cast a reassuring smile at his sister as he urged Nico out of the kitchen but Giselle presented him with a view of her back.

Definitely pissed.

What was it about tonight that was getting him into hot water with females left and right? Maybe his ex fiancée had a point when she'd told him his he-man tactics weren't going to go far with women who had any inclination to think for themselves.

Nah. She'd just been mad at the time. He could

make it up to Giselle and he'd figure out a way to make it up to Esme tomorrow. He hoped.

"I mean it, Renzo, we've got to do something about convincing Giselle to get the hell out of this business." Nico fumed as he stalked down the hall away from the kitchen. "She should be thinking about getting married, not getting laid. What is it with all the do-me erotic artwork and now the porno doughnuts? Jesus, we have to convince her to take her cooking somewhere else."

"Could we just handle one family crisis at a time? Right now we need to worry more about how Marco is going to get through law school. He called me tonight and apparently we've got another cash flow problem." The youngest Cesare had started at Harvard two months ago and the effort to keep him in the prestigious school was costing the family big-time.

Renzo found an exit to the beach on the rear wall of the corridor outside Club Paradise's main kitchen and shouldered the door open. The warm night air blew over them, the scent of the ocean bringing reassuring peace after the tension in the kitchen.

Damn but he wished he was still in Esme's bed right now. The night had taken a serious nosedive since she'd kicked him out.

"Don't tell me that school thinks it can bleed us more. I've lost track of how many checks we've written—"

"It's not the school this time." Renzo moved to the edge of the deck behind the hotel and hoisted himself to sit on the wooden railing, thinking the night air would feel even better if he was sharing it with a delicate blonde instead of his cranky older brother. "It's that piece of crap car he was driving which a local mechanic declared DOA after it broke down on the interstate. He's going to need something else to get him around town."

"Shit."

"My sentiments exactly."

"You know I'm only making a fraction of what I used to now that I've moved to coaching?" Nico shook his head, frustration written in every tense line of his pacing gait. "I know it's still a hell of a lot more than most people make, but—"

But Nico had gotten sucked into living large and now he had bills ten times higher than he could afford.

Which left Renzo to buy a new car for their brother.

"Actually, I think I've got a plan this time." A really ridiculous plan, maybe, but it guaranteed him a chance to see Esmerelda Giles again.

He breathed in the salty ocean breeze and took comfort in the soft swish of the water hitting the shore beyond the deck area.

Nico quit pacing. "I'll come up with my half. If only I could unload that damn house of mine I could make all this go away in a heartbeat."

"Don't worry about it." The more he thought about this plan—and the fact that Esme was probably in the market for a new job anyway—the more Renzo couldn't wait for morning to come so he could talk to her about it. "I've been meaning to develop a new business with a higher profit margin and I think I've finally figured out what to do."

First thing tomorrow he'd make Esme a business proposition she couldn't refuse—a plan that would bode well for them both professionally.

As for their personal relationship, he didn't kid himself that he'd find his way back into her bed again any time soon. But he could be a patient man when he wanted something badly enough.

And where there was a will...

5

THERE *HAD* TO BE a way.

Esme stared down at her checkbook balance the next morning and wondered how she could possibly pay for this sensual, exotic hotel suite out of her own pocket. Sure, her lovely neighbor Mrs. Wolcott had held the room on her credit card and would automatically be billed if Esme didn't pay for it, but how could she allow her friend to finance something so extravagant when she hadn't even had the courtesy to show up for her date with the woman's nephew?

Sighing, she juggled the hotel phone from one ear to another while she waited for the automated voice on the other end that would inform her of her credit-card balance and how much room she had left on the account.

As if she didn't already know.

Ever since her car had been repossessed, she'd been painfully aware of the dwindling amount in her checking account.

Gazing around at her lush surroundings, Esme soaked up the fine details with an appreciative eye. The tent effect of the taupe-colored linen draped overhead conveyed a warm intimacy even in the sprawling suite. The constant soft gurgle of the brook winding through the living area to finally drain into a grate along the bathroom floor provided a soothing white noise that relaxed her despite the enormous stress of being unemployed, in debt and deprived of transportation.

Sinking deeper into the wing-back chair beside the neoclassical mahogany desk, Esme returned the phone to its cradle, assured she couldn't possibly pay for the hotel room and still eat for the next week.

Damn Renzo Cesare.

She might have been more inclined to enjoy eating rice for the next seven days if she'd at least had the pleasure of sleeping with him last night. Then she could have justified the astronomical cost for this fantastic room because she would have had delicious memories to tide her over.

But now, she was certain to resent every bite of rice since she'd been deprived of fantastic sex last night, and she'd be deprived of pizza and chocolate next week.

Frustrated on every level, Esme didn't appreciate the knock on the door that interrupted her brooding. Didn't housekeeping have any other rooms to clean? Empty rooms rented by people who actually had a life?

Grumbling her way to the door, she shoved up her sleeve to check the hour on her heavy silver timepiece. Eleven-thirty. Since she'd asked for a late checkout, that meant she still had over an hour to hang out and enjoy the atmosphere of the room.

She tugged open the door, prepared to ask the maid to come back later.

"Morning." The six-foot plus, smiling stud in her doorway was definitely not a maid.

No, the dark-haired, muscle-bound male exuding a lethal combination of pheromones and testosterone was more likely to rumple her sheets than make her bed. Not that she would let him.

But she'd be lying through her teeth if she said she wasn't just a little excited to see him.

"Renzo." Too late she realized she'd huffed out the name with too much breathless anticipation when she *soo* could not afford to be attracted to him. Willing away the relentless thrill tripping through her, she straightened. "I'm sorry if I gave you the wrong impression last night, but I don't think we should—"

"I understand completely." He held up a hand as if to ward off any other objections, his broad chest flexing against the gray Cesare Construction T-shirt he wore tucked into a pair of jeans that would make any woman look twice. "I'm here with more of a business proposition than a personal one."

"You're here on business?" She couldn't imagine what they could possibly have to discuss in that realm. "I don't know what you have in mind, but I don't think I could ever do business with someone I can't trust."

"Don't you think you're being a little hard on me,

Esme? I've admitted I was out of line by lying to you, but you have to know it was never my intention to set foot in your room last night. I only meant to walk you up here to be sure you were safe."

But then new Esme and her plans for seduction had enticed him inside. Wincing, she remembered his reluctance, but she hadn't twisted his arm either. "And then I dragged poor unsuspecting you into my lair to seduce you, right? Sorry, Renzo, but I'm not taking the blame for last night."

She'd shouldered enough blame for the incident with Miles Crandall, her touchy-feely boss at the museum, when she hadn't done a damn thing to mislead him. She wasn't about to let Renzo make her out as a culprit in his scheme.

He shook his head, freeing a lock of dark hair to fall along his brow. "You're a lot tougher than you look, Esme Giles, I'll grant you that much. Are you sure I couldn't talk to you for fifteen minutes this morning? I came up with a hell of an idea that could be profitable for us both."

She stared into those endlessly brown eyes of his and found herself wanting to believe him. He *had* possessed enough courtesy to at least own up to the truth last night before finishing. A lot of guys would have taken what they wanted and worried about the ethics of the situation later.

Besides, who was she to turn away any business propositions given the state of her finances and her shredded career?

"It's just business?" She needed this clarified up front. Even if she'd dreamed of the man's kisses all night, that didn't mean she would be willing to accept any romantic overtures from him in the future. He hadn't proven himself at all trustworthy in that department.

"Just business." He crossed his heart like an earnest eight-year-old.

The absurdity of the gesture coming from a man who looked as though he probably weight-lifted eight-year-olds in his spare time made her smile in spite of herself.

"We can go down to the lobby to talk if you'd feel more comfortable," he offered, stepping backward in the corridor as if to make way for her to join him.

Esme opened the door wider, giving in to the persistence of the man. "That's okay. If you were going to rob me and leave me for dead it would have been a much easier job last night while I was throwing myself at you."

She tried not to notice the sudden charge in the air as he entered her suite for the second time in twenty-four hours. The atmosphere grew thicker, heavy with awareness.

An awareness she wouldn't acknowledge, by God. Not after the way he'd misled her just for kicks.

She led them toward two low-slung chairs positioned close enough to the narrow, manmade brook that guests could dip their toes in the water if they were so inclined.

Which Esme wasn't. She didn't trust herself to remove so much as a sandal in this man's presence for fear once she started taking off things she wouldn't be able to stop.

"Thanks for letting me in." Renzo stood behind one of the chairs and waited while she took her seat.

For a South Beach player who liked to toy with unsuspecting women, he sure had nice manners.

"You must know any hint of profitability is an irresistible lure to an unemployed woman." She couldn't help but enjoy the play of muscles against his clothes as he lowered himself into the seat across from her. "But it occurs to me I don't even know what line of work you're in since I thought you were Hugh the journalist last night."

"Cesare Construction." He scrubbed a hand across the T-shirt that proclaimed as much, drawing her attention back to the impressive chest she'd be better off not noticing. "I make a lot of cabinets personally, but I also oversee crews at various jobs around town, building everything from houses to gazebos. It's probably not as exciting as journalism, but it was my father's business."

"And I'm sure it's a profitable one for *you*, but I can't imagine someone like *me* wielding a hammer anytime soon."

Although the image of Renzo in a tool belt working up a sweat was enough to make a woman contemplate donning a hardhat.

He leaned forward in his seat, pinning her with

those dark eyes of his as he braced his elbows on his sprawling knees. "I was thinking more about what you said in regard to the market for antique reproductions, remember?"

She nodded. "I guess I still don't see the connection though. What does the antique market have to do with building gazebos?"

"I can make reproductions as good as anything you see in this room." He made a sweeping gesture to include the darkly unique neoclassical pieces that had delighted her. "If you can find buyers for that sort of thing, we might have a very viable business on our hands."

She stared at the small table with the embroidered insert beneath its glass top and then glanced back to Renzo's construction T-shirt. "It's much more difficult than you might think to give the pieces the proper aged look. Creating reproductions is an art that takes trained furniture makers many years to perfect."

"I've got rooms full of stuff like this that I've made. If you don't think it's good enough, obviously, the deal's off." He shrugged with the blasé attitude that could only come with total confidence.

Hadn't he surprised her last night by being able to pinpoint the style of the pieces?

"You already have some pieces completed?" The flea-market fanatic within her awoke. She'd been lured to estate sales and bargain basements all over Florida to seek out hidden treasures on fewer assurances than this. What would it hurt to see what sorts of things Renzo had crafted?

"I've got an attic full of oddball pieces I made for kicks." He leaned to one side in his seat and reached to skim his fingers along the surface of the water that gurgled past them in the manmade stream. "Whenever the thought of putting together another set of cabinets starts to feel a little monotonous, I like working on a Shaker chair or an oversized Colonial table—something really different."

Esme resisted the urge to fan herself. She knew her passion for antique furniture went beyond the average Saturday garage-sale shopper's, but the thought of getting her hands on some quality reproductions seriously pushed all her buttons.

"Do you have time to show me the pieces today?" As an out-of-work art historian, her time was all her own.

Grinning, Renzo righted himself in the chair, gently shaking the water from his fingers. "Are you going to consider my proposition?"

Distracted by his glistening hand, she couldn't help but wonder what it might feel like if he were to trail those damp fingers over her bare skin. Between her breasts. Down the center of her belly to her...

"Esme?"

She blinked. Dragged her thoughts back to business. Chairs. Tables. Profits.

"Let's just see what the pieces look like and then we'll go from there." The clients she occasionally worked with through the museum had very exacting standards. She rose to her feet, eager to set aside thoughts of Renzo's hands on her body. She needed to view his work and judge it for herself. "But assuming the quality is there, I'd say we have a deal."

No matter what her personal feelings might be for Renzo Cesare—and Esme wasn't even sure she cared to investigate that right now—she couldn't possibly refuse the chance to earn some cash while she looked for another job.

Renzo rose from his chair, his big body taking up more space than she'd counted on, putting him too close to her. He stared down at her, his warm gaze somehow keeping her near when she knew it would be wiser to step away.

"I don't suppose you'll want to seal the deal with a kiss?" His voice hit a gruff note despite his light, teasing tone.

She backed a step, her feet connecting with the chair behind her and threatening her balance.

But Renzo's hands were suddenly on her hips, steadying her. Righting her.

Oh God, she was a total twit.

Luckily, his touch evaporated almost as quickly as it had appeared, leaving Esme with just a vague sensory memory of warm palms and strong fingers.

Strange how the man whose lies had devastated her last night could also be the man who kept her on her feet—in more ways than one—this morning.

"Sorry." He held his hands up where she could see

them. The gesture of an innocent man. "The kiss comment was uncalled-for. I definitely want to work on this project with you, Esme, and I can promise I'll hold up my end of the business, but I would be lying if I said I didn't still want you."

Her heartbeat stumbled to a slow-motion pace, each thump louder than the next as those words washed over her. Still, as much as they might appeal to her wounded pride, she knew they didn't mean anything.

"Wanting" her was a guy euphemism for wanting to get laid, right? Frankly, other than her one attempt to be daring last night, she wasn't much for relationships based solely on sex.

Though God knows, if any man stood a chance at changing her mind, it just might be this one.

She eased toward the table where her checkbook still lay and scooped the remnants of the paperwork into her purse. "I appreciate your honesty this morning so I'm going to be straight with you, too. To my way of thinking, if you were really interested in any kind of relationship with me that would last more than twelve hours, you wouldn't have tried to meet me through subterfuge. So excuse me if I don't feel like flirting. I really think if we're going to work together we need to quit the whole romantic pretense, okay?"

She hefted her small overnight bag onto one shoulder, prepared to check out of the hotel.

He stalked closer, his dark eyebrows knit together as if in fierce concentration. Seemingly without thinking about it, he lifted the bag off her shoulder and tossed it easily over his own. "How about this—I agree to absolute hands-off until you tell me otherwise?"

"Until?" She rolled her eyes as she tugged open the door of the Sensualist's Suite. The man was arrogant as hell. "What makes you think I'll ever tell you otherwise?"

"Wishful thinking, I guess." He followed her out into the corridor and pushed the elevator button to take them downstairs. "Do you want to follow me in your car out to the house where I keep the furniture, or do you want to ride with me?"

RENZO HAD NOTICED Esme go completely still when he asked her that question.

Now, nearly an hour later as he drove his truck out to the family home in Coral Gables, he stole covert glances at her in the passenger seat and wondered why she'd been so hesitant.

He'd thought he was being at his non-pushy best when he'd offered for her to follow him out to Coral Gables in her car. She didn't seem all that thrilled to be riding with him, yet she'd haltingly told him that's what she would prefer since she'd apparently caught a ride out to Club Paradise in the first place.

But at least she was here. By his side.

Contemplating a business partnership with him.

He couldn't have screwed things up too badly last night if she was willing to look at his furniture with him, and that was all the encouragement he needed. He might have intercepted her last night because she looked as though she needed assistance, but he sure as hell hadn't kissed her just to be helpful.

No, Esmerelda Giles in her understated dress and bold nakedness beneath it had managed to turn him inside out with her confusing mix of feminine signals. And something about that brash determination underneath the delicate exterior thoroughly captured his attention.

Made him want to stick around long enough to figure out which Esme was real.

As he pulled into the driveway on the quiet street, he noticed her eyes narrowed, focusing on the house he'd lived in his whole life.

"This is *your* house?" Her voice registered her surprise as she took in the sprawling contemporary ranch home perched on a low rise.

"For now. My dad left it to all his kids but we took a private vote to turn it over to my oldest brother, Vito, when he returns from adventures abroad. Until then, I'm overseeing the place." He whipped the midsize pickup into one of three arched concrete carports.

"This is your family home?" She slid out the passenger door before he could open it for her, her feet carrying her to the middle of the driveway to take in the Cesare family compound with its rock facade and low peaked roof. "It's gorgeous."

"Yeah? My mother always said it was too 1960s Hollywood-tacky for her, but my dad considered it his personal palace. Now, it's just home." He waved her into the side door, the closest entrance to the climate-controlled section of the attic where he kept his furniture pieces.

"Does your mother still live here?" Esme smoothed her silky blond hair with one hand and straightened her long gauzy skirt with the other.

He probably should have just averted that inevitable question by speaking of his mom more firmly in the past tense, but no matter how long his parents had been gone, they still seemed a part of life to Renzo and his siblings. Real. Present.

"She died in childbirth after she had my youngest brother Marco. She'd been pregnant with twins and she lost the second baby—my other little sister. My father followed them twelve years ago after a heart attack. Giselle said he missed my mom too much, but who knows. My brother Vito took over parenting then." Which was why Renzo and Nico refused to ask Vito for financial help with their youngest brother now. Vito had more than served his time as head of the household.

He turned to her as he opened the door to let them in. "Whoops. Way too much information for an impersonal working relationship, right? Come on in."

She edged past him sideways in that delicate manner she had of not taking up too much space.

"I'm sorry about your folks," she murmured, meeting his eyes in a moment of quiet sympathy before turning to absorb the rest of the house. "That must have been very hard for all of you."

He shrugged past those old hurts, grateful he'd still had family to turn to despite what they'd lost. Instead, he focused on Esme, watched her as she stepped inside the kitchen, she peered all around as if cataloging every detail.

"The house *is* very sixties Hollywood." She looked back at him over one shoulder. "You know that's totally chic now?"

"Chic or not, my mom wasn't sold. She liked her more traditional house in Naples—Italy, not Florida— and this house was the epitome of American tackiness in her eyes." He opened the refrigerator and hunted for something appropriate to offer her. "I've got lemonade in a can or beer." He turned to her, one in each hand. "Not exactly a gourmet's choice, but—"

She took the can of lemonade and punctured the lid. Renzo kept the bottle of beer and twisted off the top before clinking his glass against her aluminum. "Then here's to new beginnings."

Without waiting for agreement, he led her behind the kitchen to the narrow stairs he'd built himself for quick access to the storage area. "The roof is low up here, you'll have to be careful."

She laughed as she reached the top step and entered the low overhead area. "You mean *you* have to be careful. The room feels just right to— Ohmigod."

Her eye locked on something behind him. Turning, he spied the object of her fascination—a walnut sideboard he'd built on a huge scale that didn't exactly have great practical application. Running almost the length of the whole space, the giant piece was one of the few furnishings that he hadn't covered with a dust cloth and it probably wouldn't even fit in the average American dining room.

"I know that's a little overproportioned," he admitted, scrambling to pull the protective sheets off some of the other pieces. "But I've got lots of other things that are more traditional—chairs, tables, book-shelves..."

And beds. An item he didn't mention aloud, but which remained prominent in his thoughts as he focused on Esme's slender frame amid all the heavy furniture.

"I love this." Her hand smoothed over the dark surface of the wood, around one curved corner to linger on the paneled doors. "It has a late medieval appeal. The aged look of the stain is amazing."

He dropped the armful of dust cloths he'd gathered and joined her in front of the gargantuan sideboard, close enough to catch a whiff of her perfume—something soft and maybe vanilla scented. She made quiet little exclamations of delight over every detail. The smooth operation of the hidden hinge mechanism. The genuine wood backing on the entire cabinet. The fretwork he'd carved as decoration along one edge.

The artisan within him experienced an unexpected tide of satisfaction at her approval as she noted authentic period details. The man within him wished she would trail her fingers over him the same way she caressed the polished wood.

She examined everything with the same thorough attention, feeling the flat surfaces along with the rungs and legs of various pieces. She withdrew a pad of paper from her purse and made notes on everything, praising him for minute particulars no one had ever noticed about his work before.

He could have watched her all day.

But after hours spent in close quarters with Esmerelda Giles and her sweet vanilla scent, his hands itched to touch her, to run rogue over her body like they had the night before.

For that matter, her little murmurs of joy as she discovered each new chair or shelf or—worse—each elaborate bed frame, had nudged him to the brink of insanity. They had worked side-by-side for hours in the intimacy of an attic where he couldn't even stand up straight. He could either sit back in one of the twenty-odd chairs or he could hover over her shoulder, his bent shoulders placing his nose even closer to the luscious sweetness of that soft vanilla scent and those occasional quiet gasps of pleasure.

If she could sigh with appreciation over an inanimate object, what kind of noises would she make underneath him, her legs wrapped around his waist and her head thrown back until...

"Renzo?"

He blinked away the thoughts of Esme naked, wishing he hadn't made that dumb-ass promise not to touch her unless she asked him to. How would he ever get close enough to trace the source of her scent if he couldn't touch her? "What?"

She set down her pencil and paper on a French Rococo dresser complete with gilded paint and curved drawers. "We've been working on this too long, haven't we? I tend to lose all track of time when I get involved in this sort of thing."

"So do we have a deal? We could always celebrate the beginning of a new partnership." He scooped up her notebook and automatically held out a hand to her as she sucked in a breath to squeeze between two earlier sets of cabinets he'd never been totally happy with.

Too late, he remembered the damn no-touching promise.

She held on to his extended arm for balance until she cleared the maze of furnishings, the caress of her skin against his a heated brand that sizzled right through him.

Relinquishing his fingers as if she hadn't even noticed the intimacy of the contact, she nodded.

"We definitely have a deal." Sidling past him, she picked her way down the stairs, moving in that careful, precise manner that had caught his eye last night amid the denizens of Club Paradise who prided themselves on letting it all hang out.

He followed her down to the kitchen, unwilling to part with this chance to get closer to her without necessarily touching. All he needed to do was to make her come to him.

"Excellent." He reached for a bottle of sauvignon blanc in the wine rack behind the pantry. Nothing too fancy, but it went with fish. "But it's Cesare family tradition to seal the big deals by breaking bread together."

It was true enough. He didn't need to tell her Cesare family tradition called for a big meal for most every other occasion, too.

She bit her lip as she stared up at him, her blue eyes communicating all the hesitancy she hadn't voiced yet.

Plowing ahead before she had the chance, he pulled a wineglass from the china cabinet and stuffed it in her hand. "So, what do you say, Esme? Can you forgive me enough to let me make dinner for you tonight?"

6

A NORMAL WOMAN WOULD SAY YES.

Who could resist this tall, dark and gorgeous man with a bottle of wine in hand as he promised her dinner?

"I have to admit, the offer is tempting." Her fingers flexed around the stout wineglass.

"You've put in a long day and I happen to know you couldn't have gotten much sleep last night. You owe it to yourself to let me cook for you." He cracked the seal on the wine and started peeling off the paper around the top of the bottle. "Besides, dinner is the least I can do for you after I messed up your date last night."

Which reminded her she never did make connections with her neighbor about the disastrous outcome of her date with Hugh. The day had been a blur of new worries and new hopes.

And Renzo.

"I'll stay for dinner on one condition." Determined to call a few of the shots tonight, Esme had no intention of letting her new business partner think he could maneuver her too easily. She'd been that route with her last employer and he'd walked all over her.

Still, she extended her glass to Renzo as he uncorked the wine.

"And what might that be?" He loomed closer, his broad shoulders filling too much of her line of vision, yet true to his word, he didn't touch her.

"I get to ask all the questions I want and you have to be honest about the answers." If the man lied to her again, all bets were off for this business deal.

But something inside her already seemed confident that wouldn't happen. An innate sense of honor shimmered through Renzo's actions, a definite hint of nobility that rested side-by-side with all that cocky male arrogance. She saw it in his good manners, heard it in the way he spoke about his family.

"You want to ask me questions?" He finished filling her glass and moved to pull a chair out from the kitchen table. "You probably know more about this furniture than I do, but ask away while I start dinner."

She took the seat he'd held out for her and smiled to herself as he shoved the fruit bowl spilling over with grapes closer to her fingertips. She leaned back in her chair and plucked a green grape from its stem, thinking she had a very nice view as Renzo snagged a glass for himself from the china cabinet.

Denim was invented for men like Renzo Cesare.

"My questions aren't about furniture. They're about you." She planned to be direct, honest and up front with him.

"Me?" He stalled in the middle of pouring his glass

of white wine. "I don't know that I'll make for fascinating dinner conversation, but I'm game."

"You lure me into staying for dinner with a bottle of wine in one hand and a basket of grapes in the other." She plucked another piece of green fruit from the bowl. "You're like Bacchus reincarnated and tempting me into things I know I shouldn't do, yet here I am, letting you make me dinner. I'd say you're a very interesting topic of conversation."

"Bacchus, huh?" He moved around the stovetop like a pro, looking infinitely more adept in the kitchen than she'd ever been. "The Greek god of wine and intoxication, right? If I'm remembering correctly I think he was also the god of orgies and wantonness."

She couldn't see his face as he filled a pot with water at the sink, but she detected the smile in his voice.

"The Greeks didn't have an orgy god. I definitely would have remembered if they did." It would have livened up her western civilization classes in grad school, that's for sure. "You might be confusing drunken reveling with orgies."

Turning, he lifted his glass as if to toast her from across the room. "Then let's cross our fingers one thing leads to another."

"You're already giving me trouble and I haven't even asked my first question yet." She wondered why it seemed too easy to talk to Renzo, and how her comfort with him had happened so fast. She'd worked with Miles Crandall for five years and she hadn't been at ease around him in all that time.

Renzo had blustered his way into her life with a lie and preceded to turn her life on its ear in the course of twenty-four hours, yet she never once felt nervous around him.

Maybe her instincts about men weren't as bad as she'd thought.

"Sorry. I'll keep all my hopes for a drunken revel to myself. What did you want to ask me?"

"How could you have made so much furniture at such a young age and still work at another full-time job?" She'd start with an easy question, something practical.

"I'm a classic overachiever and I don't need much sleep. Next?"

She sensed more to that story, but she didn't press. Yet.

"I lost track of all the siblings you mentioned. Can you go over the list again?" As an only child, Esme had always been fascinated by big families.

"There are five of us. Vito's the race-car driver in Europe. My brother Nico used to play for the National Hockey League, but he got hurt and now he's coaching a team. I'm next in the lineup, then Giselle, who is the executive chef for Club Paradise and made us the drinks last night. Last is my younger brother Marco—the surviving twin—who just started at Harvard Law this fall." He dumped a box of pasta into a boiling pot as the kitchen filled with the scent of seafood and garlic. "There will be a quiz on this later."

"You're lucky to have such a big family. Although I

can't imagine how your sister survived all the macho-assertive protectiveness if your brothers are anything like you."

"Actually, I think having to contend with us has just made her more determined and stubborn than the rest of us put together." He set the timer on the stove and then moved to a seat across from her at the table. He topped off both their glasses and stared at her, patient and unblinking.

Perhaps it was the wine that made her stare back a little too long. Or maybe she was just incredibly attracted to Renzo Cesare and there were no two ways around it.

Her senses swam, overloaded with the scents of melted butter and broiled shrimp, the taste of fresh grapes and mellow wine, the memory of Renzo's hands on her body and the feel of his eyes probing hers.

"Is it my turn to ask you anything yet?" His voice slid over her with the low confidentiality of pillow talk.

"I guess that would be okay." She couldn't keep him in the hot seat forever. Still, she stole a sip from her glass to steel herself.

"I know I said I wouldn't touch you unless you asked me to, and I'll live up to that promise if it kills me. But can you at least tell me if you've even thought about touching *me* at all today?"

The wine seemed to suck all the fluid from her mouth, leaving her throat too dry to respond.

Had she agreed to be honest with her answers, or was it only Renzo who had to comply with that rule?

His dark eyes observed her with clear interest, not missing a second of her hesitation. Indecision.

"I'll admit I might have thought about it a time or two." There. Honest, but light. Simple. She didn't want to dwell on the fact that she'd thought about him that way today at all, but there was no denying her fingers had ached with the need to skim those well-tooled muscles, that sun-bronzed skin. "But I think that's normal after what happened last night. I'm sure once we've been working together for a few days we'll forget all about that."

"What if we can't forget it?" He leaned across the table as if to confide a secret. "What if days go by and we think about it more instead of less?"

"That would make things difficult." She'd gotten worked up enough examining table legs with Renzo. What made her think she could somehow excise steamy thoughts of him if she engaged in private dinners with the man? "Why don't we wait and cross that bridge when we come to it?"

"We could do that." He plucked a grape from the bunch draped over the top of the fruit bowl between them and popped it in his mouth. "Or we could come up with a Plan B, just in case that doesn't work."

"Plan B?" She watched him eat another grape, her gaze drawn to his mouth.

The fearless new Esme from last night would have jumped him, but now she wrestled with old insecurities and a worry that she shouldn't mix her professional life with her personal wants. What if, having let new Esme out for a wild night on the town, she could never subvert that bold part of her soul again?

"It's always good to have a backup, don't you think? If we're still thinking about slow, deep kisses every time we're together by next week, we ought to figure out what we're going to do about it."

Her heart picked up rhythm at the words. Right now, she couldn't picture ever looking at Renzo and not thinking about lingering, searching kisses. As she stared at the strong column of his throat while he swallowed another sip of his wine, Esme imagined how he would taste right now.

She stifled the urge to lick her lips. "I can't imagine what we would do. I have to admit it's a bit of a distraction."

A delicious distraction, but still...

"I vote if it gets too distracting, we just act on it." He held out a grape to her, his hand hovering a few inches from her mouth.

Parting her lips for this man would be dangerous. She accepted his offering with her fingers, however, and tasted the grape on her tongue.

Renzo would have tasted better.

"Act on it?" Perhaps she needed to give the idea some thought. A woman couldn't deny her urges forever, after all.

"Sure. Maybe if we just gave in to the desire it

would settle down again. Sort of a last-ditch attempt to get it out of our systems.''

Renzo expected her to call him on the carpet at any moment for his incendiary suggestion. And part of him longed for her to do just that. He'd always been a man of action, ready to take charge, make things happen. He wouldn't mind getting all the chemistry between them out in the open.

But dinner passed, hours passed, and she hadn't pointed a finger at him for making self-serving suggestions while she'd been slightly under the influence.

They had set up a plan for working together, had agreed to maintain autonomy in their areas of expertise—his in building, hers in client contact—and had made plans to draw up a formal contract with the help of a lawyer.

But they hadn't gotten back to the topic that intrigued him most of all. How would they handle the undeniable attraction that flared to life whenever they moved within fifty yards of one another?

Now, as he drove her back home to an apartment complex on Miami Beach, just north of the South Beach strip, he couldn't dance around the heat between them anymore.

The suspense was killing him.

Her vanilla scent teased his nose in the intimacy of the truck cab while the shoulder bared by her silky tank top loomed within reach if only he could reach out and touch her.

She'd been silent for so long, Renzo couldn't take it another minute.

"You're awfully quiet over there." The subtle probe for information marked a first for him. He couldn't remember ever having to ask a woman what she was thinking before. Either the women he'd been with had shared their thoughts or—much scarier—he hadn't ever cared enough to solicit more information. "You having second thoughts about the business?"

About him.

"Just thinking." She wrenched her gaze from whatever had preoccupied her out the window. She gave him one of those rusty Esme smiles before turning her attention back to the city lights winking on the intercoastal water as they crossed one of the causeways out to Miami Beach.

Thinking?

Never having been a patient person, Renzo gave up on subtlety.

"I guess I was wondering *what* you were thinking," he clarified, drumming his thumbs on the steering wheel in time to the jazz music drifting through the dashboard speakers. "In my family we talk while we're thinking. And we talk while we're disagreeing, while we're negotiating, while we're wheedling... There's talking going on pretty much nonstop. I don't know what to make of this quiet thinking business."

Esme swiveled toward him, readjusting her seat belt so she could tuck her feet up under her, her long gauzy skirt flowing over slender legs and spilling to the floor.

Renzo had the sense that she was preparing herself—finally—to talk to him and he made a mental note not to interrupt.

"Remember when we were talking right before dinner tonight and you asked me what we would do if we couldn't...you know...forget about the kisses we'd shared?" The color in her cheeks heightened just a little, but she watched him steadily, her blue eyes seemingly calculating his response.

"Hell yeah, I remember." Despite all their talk about business, he'd either been thinking of that conversation or the kisses themselves in the back of his mind all evening. "I realize that was presumptuous of me, but I—"

Recalling his resolution not to interrupt, he stopped himself before he went any further. "Why?"

"Well, I've been giving that idea a lot of thought." She peered out the windshield as he turned down Lincoln Road. "My apartment building is on the left just after that next stop sign."

Renzo waited. Strained for a hint of what she might be driving at in the tone of her voice and came up empty. He was definitely no expert on deciphering women. He spent most of his days hanging out with construction crews whose idea of getting females involved whistling at women on the street. Of course he didn't have a clue about cross-gender communication.

He parked the truck in the driveway of the apart-

ment complex she pointed out and hustled to open her
door for her. The low stucco building couldn't have
held more than eight apartments, but it boasted a
lighted swimming pool alongside the parking area,
surrounded by a few low palm trees to provide some
shade. By the illumination of the street lamps, he
could see each apartment had its own patio, some
overflowing with healthy tropical plants or bright
lawn furniture, others devoid of any decoration.

Vaguely he wondered which one belonged to Esme.
More importantly, he wondered what she might have
to say on the topic of kissing.

"You've been thinking?" he prodded as he helped
her down from the truck cab and onto the sidewalk in
front of the building.

He didn't want her to slip into her apartment without him before they finished their discussion.

"Yes." A gentle night breeze blew a strand of her
long blond hair across her neck, ruffled the hem of her
thin skirt. "The idea of our partnership crashing and
burning because we're too caught up in thinking
about what might have been doesn't sit well with me.
I'll admit I was too distracted to think clearly when we
were going over some of the general contractual
points of our agreement, and I don't want to make a
mistake just because of simple chemistry."

Renzo felt his eyes widen to the saucer-round pro-
portions of Saturday morning cartoon characters.
She'd been distracted? Ms. Cultured Art Historian
with the no-nonsense long skirt who'd spent most of

the evening with a pencil tucked into her hair to keep the silky strands out of her face?

She'd done a hell of a job hiding it.

Confused, he couldn't help but quiz her to figure out exactly what she meant. "You mean you're having reservations about us doing business together? Or are you suggesting we move ahead with..." Hope surged inside him along with new fire in his veins. "Plan B?"

His throat ran dry at the very idea while the sultry breeze blew around them, toying with her skirt hem.

"First, let me just say that I want to move ahead with the business." Her blue eyes projected a fiery determination while her voice held a note of absolute certainty. "Are you sure you can be committed to our work together no matter what sort of turn our personal lives might take?"

Her soft pink mouth seemed to invite his kiss more than conversation. He struggled against the urge to lean in and take what he wanted, drag her into her apartment and make love to her until they couldn't dance around each other with indecision any longer.

His fingers flexed, clenched at his sides to keep from touching her. If she'd put this many hours of thought into her words, he'd damn well pay her the courtesy of listening.

"I'll be honest with you, Esme. I *need* this business to work out. I've got bills to pay that require success, the sooner the better."

She nodded with slow satisfaction. And, it seemed to Renzo, new resolution.

"Then I'm in favor of a Plan C that I've mapped out on my own. May I share it with you?"

Plan C? He had himself so worked up at the thought of her actually biting on Plan B—the one which involved more kissing her strawberry-lip-gloss-flavored mouth, more touching her silky-soft skin—that he almost couldn't nudge an acknowledgement past his lips now.

"Plan C, huh?" He liked making all the plans, damn it. "Definitely. Let's hear what you have in mind."

He knew she couldn't have missed the disappointment in his voice. He'd never been the kind of guy who masked his emotions, so when he did now, he was probably about as transparent as the polyurethane finish he used on his furniture creations.

Undaunted, Esme took a step closer to him, smack dab into his personal space. Near enough for him to breathe in the fragrance of her sweet scent, near enough for him to feel the warmth of her body inches away from his.

She splayed her palms across his chest, right over the place where his heart slammed a hungry beat. Licking her lips with a quick dart of her pink tongue she leaned close enough for her whisper to float on the balmy breeze.

"Plan C is we don't stop at just kissing."

7

ESME FEARED she wouldn't be able to hear Renzo's answer given that her heartbeat thundered in her ears with all the force of the "1812 Overture."

And although she'd been telling herself that she needed to be more aggressive about going after what she wanted in life rather than simply hoping for the best, she had chosen a risky mission for this first foray into the pursuit of her goals. Renzo Cesare had provided her with a demoralizing setback yesterday. And although she'd be even more humiliated if he was still playing games with her now, that high-risk factor also made him all the more appealing.

If she could face rejection from Renzo and move on to a strictly business relationship with him, wouldn't that be resounding proof of her new attitude? Assuming, of course, she survived the experience.

Now, her talkative new business partner who always seemed to know his own mind stared at her with unmasked surprise.

Shaking his head, he closed his eyes for a moment, his long dark lashes brushing the bronze skin of his cheekbones.

"Normally, Esme, I'm a man of action. I don't usually weigh the consequences before I act, and I follow my instincts on everything from how to cut a piece of wood to how I approach a woman I'm attracted to." He slid her overnight bag off his shoulder and dropped it on the sidewalk. Still, he didn't reach for her, didn't plant his hands on her body the way she wanted him to. "And I want you to know that if I listened to my instincts right now, we'd already be headed for your bedroom."

Esme's breath caught in her throat at the vision of her and Renzo tangled around each other, her fingers sinking into his shoulders as they fell into her crisp cotton sheets.

"But you've decided not to follow your instincts when it comes to me?" That was great. Just great. She really knew how to bring out the animal in a man.

"Not necessarily." He reached out to smooth a strand of her hair between two fingers. "But today I watched the way you look things over, study all the angles and think about them before you make a decision. After how I pushed you to a wall last night, I just want to be damn sure I'm not pressuring you this time."

A shiver trembled through her at his touch.

"I'd rather have you help me follow my instincts." She needed the kind of confidence he had, craved the self-assurance evident in every move he made. "Your approach sounds a lot more enticing than mine right now."

"That's just it. You're thinking about right now.

What about the reality of working together tomorrow?'' His hand skimmed her cheek, grazed her temple.

Memories of their bodies entwined on the hotel bed last night made her tilt her head into his touch, craving a deeper caress.

"I've spent my whole life looking out for tomorrow and you know where it's gotten me?''

He shook his head. Of course he couldn't know what that would be like.

"I've worried myself <u>into</u> a suffocating little corner. And the worst part of it was finding out that even my narrow corner wasn't safe. I didn't have the pleasure of taking any exciting risks and I ended up getting screwed anyway.'' She shrugged, not meaning to sound bitter. "Now I'm ready to take the risks, not worry about the consequences, and to be perfectly honest, I'm crossing my fingers I'll be rewarded with a nominal sensual payoff.''

"Nominal?'' The hand that had been smoothing over her cheek stilled. Tensed. He bent his head as if to kiss her and her eyes fluttered closed.

Instead of brushing her lips, however, his mouth grazed her ear as he whispered, "I suggest you find your keys, Esme, and we'll see about nominal. You obviously have no idea who you're dealing with.''

Sensation tingled through her, a warm flush of anticipation that made her skin tighten into chill bumps. A rush of satisfaction coursed through her at the idea she had successfully goaded him, teased him into pleasing her.

Fishing her keys from a side pocket of her overnight bag, she led him over the patio of her ground-floor apartment and unlocked the sliding glass door surrounded by plants and flowers stuffed in everything from antique teapots to turn-of-the-century apothecary bowls. Her attempts at gardening were as mishmash and disorganized as the rest of her life.

Still, the fact that she'd managed to lure a brawny stud back to her apartment galvanized her, put a little oomph into her step. She turned to him once they were safely inside her living room, the sliding door locked behind them as she searched for the right come-on line.

She needn't have bothered.

Renzo was suddenly right there, in front of her, reaching for her. She had a scant instant to witness the commitment to his cause in his dark eyes before his mouth came down on hers for a hard, demanding kiss.

The man of action had stepped to the fore.

Her keys fell from her hand as her arms went round his neck, his fingers already plowing across her back to draw her near. Her lips parted beneath his, eager to receive the kiss while her head tipped back to accommodate him.

The silky tank top she wore couldn't begin to disguise the feel of his chest against hers. If anything the layer of skimpy silk only intensified the fiery heat spiking through her at his touch.

It had been so long since a man had held her this way. And yet, no man had ever held her quite like Renzo did now, as if he couldn't get enough of her, as if he had to have her.

Maybe this time would be better than her long-ago attempts at lovemaking. Better than nominal. Heaven knew, the preliminaries were scorching her senses and threatening to incinerate her if she didn't feel his bare skin soon.

She reached for the hem of his T-shirt as Renzo walked them deeper into her apartment, down the hallway, toward her bedroom. She couldn't wait.

Shoving up the cotton fabric with her hands, she laid her hands across the taut muscles of his chest, down the hard ripples of his abs. Her throaty moan mingled with his, and his forward momentum toward the bedroom halted. He settled for simply backing her against the hallway wall, the protruding chair rail scraping along her back only a mild annoyance compared to the absolute pleasure of having unveiled his body.

In the nanosecond it took for him to peel the shirt over his head, Esme gained a peek of smooth bronze skin in the dim light cast from the fish tank that burbled in her living room. Had she thought him worthy of a calendar page? She'd underestimated the raw sex appeal of the man. He was prime centerfold material with his sinewy arms, broad shoulders and a chest that tapered down to...

She couldn't wait to see what else.

Feeling his eyes upon hers, her gaze moved up to his. The intensity of his stare surprised her, thrilled her. Her insides smoldered with the want of him and she reached out to pull him back to her.

He lowered his mouth to hers, covered her lips to taste and tease her. His tongue slid over hers with possessive thoroughness. Desire pooled in her belly, flooded through her thighs.

"I want you." She whispered the words against his mouth, confided the truth that had been chasing around her brain for hours. She hadn't been sure she would reveal that secret, but now no matter what the cost, she wanted to take this risk with him. Needed to absorb all the pleasure he could bring her, even if the experience was fleeting.

Renzo savored Esme's every response, relished the primal simplicity of her statement.

I want you.

He growled low in his throat, his lone nod to the fierce hunger within him that craved complete possession. Last night he had stopped himself even though Esme had wanted more. He'd never find that kind of self-control two nights in a row. Not when the woman in question seduced his mind as much as his body.

Esme appealed to him on every imaginable level.

She looked so delicate standing in his shadow, her fair hair catching the scant light cast from a fish tank he'd noticed in her living room. He skimmed his hands down her bare shoulders to her waist, molded the thin fabric of her tank top to the warm skin beneath.

Her soft sighs encouraged him, made his hands work faster to free her from the silky material that separated them. Lifting the hem up, he exposed the pale skin of her belly and the soft pink lace of a bra so sheer it was almost transparent. Tight rosy nipples thrust up against the garment, plainly seeking his attention. His mouth.

He bent to kiss the soft mounds of her breasts as he tugged her blouse free. Finally he found the source of her sweet vanilla scent tucked into the slight dip of her cleavage. He licked the place with his tongue, inhaling the fragrance deeply as it intensified.

His hands cupped the curves defined by the lacy pink bra, drawing first one tight crest and then the other closer to his lips so he could taste her through the fabric. Her fingers threaded through his hair, holding him to her, steadying the pressure of his mouth. Just knowing she wanted his kiss that badly excited him all the more. He flicked open the front clasp of the bra, releasing her to his ready hands.

She was so perfect.

Her breath came in soft little pants, her fingers flying over his bare back with restless hunger. Need.

Hips twisting up against his, she wriggled as close to him as possible. His thigh slid in between hers, the denim covering his leg doing little to mask the heat of her feminine center pressed so sweetly against him.

She was turning him inside out and he hadn't even finished undressing her yet. It made no sense that Esmerelda Giles with her innocent ways, wide eyes and penchant for blind dates could get under his skin this way. He'd been with women more sophisticated, more beautiful and almost assuredly more erotically accomplished, yet he couldn't remember craving any of them the way he wanted Esme.

Sliding his hand down the slight curve of one hip, he skimmed over the front of her thigh and let his fingers start walking over the material of her long, filmy skirt. As his fingers walked south, they hiked up her skirt—inch by delicious inch. He unveiled her taut calves, her knees, the bare thighs he couldn't wait to spread wide.

Finally, when his one arm overflowed with the length of her skirt, he glimpsed the pink lace of her panties. For such a frothy piece of delicate material, those pink panties delivered a provocative punch.

He reached to touch, to graze his fingers over the sheer fabric and absorb her damp heat. She whimpered, her grip tightening on his arms.

Oh yeah.

Blood whooshed through his veins with molten force. He wanted to be inside her now. Five minutes ago. Yesterday.

He splayed his fingers wide between her legs, pressing against her thighs, the lacy edges of her panties and the sweet folds of her sex hidden beneath pink lace. He dipped one finger below the material, circled the throbbing heart of her as her knees buckled.

She fell into him, the wall behind her not nearly enough to keep her upright. He would have found immense male satisfaction in that if he didn't need her so badly at that moment.

Anchoring her with one arm against his body he lifted her, yanking the skirt and the pink lace down her quivering thighs and off her legs. She must have stepped out of her sandals on the way into the house because they were nowhere in sight.

He reached around her hips to steady her body, savoring the exquisite brush of her nakedness against him. Surely there was a bed nearby, but the first piece of furniture that caught his eye was a flat cherry sofa table polished to a dull gleam even in the faint blue light from the fish tank. A few candles decorated the surface.

Renzo seated her on the narrow table, leaned her back against the wood with a kiss more thorough, more possessive than any he'd given her yet.

Esme surprised him by pulling him down to her, her tongue meeting his with lush abandon. Her back arched off the table, her breasts flattening against him while those taut nipples teased him into paying attention.

Lowering his head to draw her into his mouth, he allowed his fingers to search through the damp curls of her sex, to hone in on the throbbing heart of her. As he stood between her spread thighs, her knees squeezed his hips, her legs drawing him closer with their restless movements.

He wanted to be inside her so badly it hurt, but he also knew once he sheathed himself in her tight heat, he would be hard pressed not to go hurtling over the edge at light speed. If he wanted to ensure her complete satisfaction, he needed to help her find it soon. Now.

She broke their kiss long enough to reach for his zipper, to drag it down and release him from his denim captivity. Her fingers brushed the fly of his cotton boxers and sent heat leaping through him.

"Wait." He held her wrist, halted the progress of the touch he'd dreamed about last night. This morning. "I want you too much already. Let me touch you."

He relaxed his hold as he met her dazed stare, her blue eyes smoky with passion.

"Is that okay, Esme?" He slid one finger inside her, felt her whole body shudder. "Can I make you see stars?"

Esme blinked past the light already dancing through her vision.

Her skin flushed hot and her nerves sang with a pleasure she'd never known. Renzo's fingers wrought delicious magic that reverberated throughout her whole body and more than anything she wanted to feel him deep inside her. A part of her.

"I can touch you, and you can tell me what you

like." He stroked a thumb over her mouth, pressing lightly on the soft fullness of her lower lip. His other hand mirrored the action between her thighs. "I want to know just what you like, Esme."

She cried out with the sharp pleasure of his touch, the sweet torment of his strong fingers. But she knew she couldn't give him what he sought.

"I don't usually—" She twitched beneath the wicked delight of his touch. "That is, I've never been able to—" She sucked on the thumb that teased her mouth, nipped him lightly with her teeth before letting him go. "Frankly, Renzo, I don't really see stars with a man."

She'd reconciled herself to the fact long ago. That didn't mean she didn't enjoy sex.

Especially sex with a man who kissed like Renzo.

"You will with me." He slid his finger deep inside her and teased one taut nipple with his other hand. "Keep your eyes open. You're not going to want to miss the show."

A damned arrogant thing to suggest. Except that, as if on cue, an electric current buzzed between the places he touched. She trembled with the shock wave of pleasure.

"You like that, Esme?" His dark eyes watched her steadily. "Then I bet you'll like this even more."

He bent to kiss the peak of her breast, to trace damp circles around the sensitive skin with his tongue, to lap at her with careful thoroughness. All the while, his fingers plied her sex with the same teasing motion around and around until...

Pleasure seized her, held her, then flooded through her whole body in a tidal wave that kept pulling her under for more and more.

She lay back on the sofa table, a piece of furniture she'd never be able to look at the same way again, awareness flitting back to her by slow degrees. When she finally propped herself up on an elbow, she was fully prepared to lavish every kind of sensual attention she could dream up on the man who had just shown her the light—stars, comets and all.

But as she met Renzo's intense gaze once again, she remembered he hadn't just enjoyed the overflow of pleasure she had. He wasn't ready for sensual teasing. No, judging by the fact that he was now totally naked, hard as steel and sheathed in a condom he must have scavenged from some secret stash of his own, Esme guessed he only wanted one thing right now.

The thought that this big, gorgeous man wanted her sent another kind of pleasure floating through her. He entered her in one swift stroke, filling and stretching her until her nails flexed into his shoulder involuntarily. He pulled back to stare down at her, study her.

"Are you okay? Esme?"

Her pulse fluttered wildly at the tender concern in his voice and she told herself not to overthink what they were doing. It was sex.

Phenomenal sex, but just sex nevertheless.

And she planned to enjoy every heady second of it.

"I'm fine. Better than fine." She gripped the hard muscles of his buttocks and pulled his hips back to hers. "I want all of you."

Renzo met her demand over and over again, filling her more completely than ever before. His release shook the rest of the candles off the table, shook her to her core.

He carried her into the bedroom after that, and he made love to her again. And again.

Each time he sought new ways to make her reach the peak she never thought she could with a man. Each time she shoved aside any thought of the consequences of her night with Renzo. He could be her business partner in the morning.

Tonight, he was the most amazing lover she would ever have. And as night stretched into morning, she told herself she could allow the indulgence of lying beside him in the warm intimacy of her bedroom even after they'd quit making love. The heaven of having a hard male body beside hers in bed was another pleasure she hadn't given herself in years. Surely it would be okay to revel in this temporary bliss.

She could close her eyes for a few minutes and simply enjoy the moment.

8

ESME HAD THE FEELING her few minutes had turned into quite a few hours when she pried an eyelid open to an obnoxious amount of sunshine streaming in through the aged vinyl blinds that covered her bedroom window.

Her hand flew to the other side of her bed before she'd even decided whether she wanted to find a man over there or not.

Empty.

A peculiar blend of disappointment and relief settled over her as she set a tentative foot on the tan industrial carpet that covered every room but the kitchen and bathroom. Her job had never paid her big bucks in the first place, but she hadn't chosen her field because she needed lush surroundings. Her apartment had a great location, nice neighbors, and she felt safe here. It worked for her. So much so that she'd gladly stopped making payments on her car so that she'd have enough money for the next few months' rent.

Transportation was a luxury she could manage without.

Housing was not.

Surprised to discover her legs still functioned despite the most enthusiastic workout she'd ever given them, Esme stepped over to her bureau and hauled out a pair of yellow satin boxer shorts and an ancient T-shirt from her sorority days that read Geeky and Grateful. Perfect comfort clothes after the most adventurous night of her life.

Ignoring the slight pang in her chest that Renzo had left without saying goodbye, Esme brushed her teeth in the so-called master bathroom off her bedroom that was no bigger than a closet, and told herself his leaving had been a good thing.

No doubt, this morning would have been very awkward. And worse, them waking up together somehow put their relationship on a much more serious footing than she'd wanted. Bad enough she couldn't resist the man who was to be her business partner. Struggling through morning-after mind games would have been too brutal for a woman so new to this taking risks thing.

As she twisted her hair into a ponytail and stuffed it in a yellow scrunchy, she reminded herself she planned to have a new attitude in her too-sheltered life anyhow. No time like the present to revel in her new sensual liberation and boldly move on after her wild encounter with Renzo.

Who had given her honest-to-God orgasms.

A guttural male curse from the next room halted the flow of heated memories.

She jumped. Squealed. Dropped her hairbrush.

"Renzo?" Her voice barely squeaked out the question in her surprise.

She waited tentatively for a reply. As if an intruder would really identify himself for her.

Opening the door of her bedroom, she strode down the few steps to the living area where the voice had come from. She found Renzo juggling two remote controls, pushing buttons relentlessly as he pointed both at her television.

"Did I wake you?" He shoved to his feet, never dropping the remotes. "Sorry about that. I nearly had everything working here when I realized the clock on the VCR still wasn't set."

Her heart thrummed too fast at the sight of him. He looked bigger, bolder, badder than yesterday, a phenomenon possibly triggered by his dark, unshaven jaw. He still wore his Cesare Construction shirt and jeans, but he must have showered because his hair lay damp and even darker than normal over his forehead.

"There." Apparently satisfied with whatever he'd accomplished with his remote control buttons, he put down the controls and gave her his undivided attention. The undiluted gaze of his intensely brown eyes. "Morning."

Esme felt his stare all the way to her most tender flesh, still tingling from last night's pleasures. With the experience of having spent a night with him, Esme knew he would kiss her, could almost taste his mouth on hers already.

But if she let that kiss happen, she'd be well on her

way to needing him. To growing addicted to those mind-drugging moments.

She couldn't afford that. Not with her life already whirling out of control in the wake of all she'd lost.

Spinning on her heel, she forced herself to walk away from the heady lure of Renzo's gaze, the air that already crackled with awareness between them.

"You don't need the remotes for the TV, by the way," she blurted, latching on to the first thing that caught her eye for a distraction. "I make sure to buy all appliances with well-marked, obvious buttons on them so I never have to rely on a remote control."

Although when she hit the button on the front of her television, the stations didn't pop onto the screen as usual.

A measured beat passed. She could practically feel his curious gaze boring into her shoulder blades, willing her to give him answers she didn't have about what last night had meant.

Finally, he cleared his throat. Stalked closer.

"That's because I set up all your channels to operate through your VCR." Was it possible his broad chest puffed out just a little more? "You'd never be able to record anything on the VCR unless you have it coordinated to be compatible with the television."

Say thank you. Just say thank you and move on.

"I don't need the VCR to record anything," she found herself saying anyway, knowing she was destined to lose both remote controls within the week. "I only use it to watch movie rentals."

She had a date with Cary Grant tonight, as a matter of fact. Emphasis on the *had*.

She had the distinct impression she'd never be able to operate her TV or VCR again without a great deal of headache. Could she help it if she wasn't technically inclined?

"Then all you do is put in the tape and hit play," Renzo assured her as he scooped up the sleek black remotes from her makeshift coffee table that was actually a stack of books. "Make sure the TV is on channel three and the VCR is— Well, look." He flashed one of the remotes in front of her nose. "—just press these two buttons and you're all set."

Peachy.

He'd been in her house for all of twelve hours and already she was losing control of her domain. Hadn't she promised herself she was going to take charge of her life in the wake of being manhandled by her boss?

Time to reassert herself, damn it.

"That's great," she lied, moving toward the kitchen as she managed a false smile. "Thanks for tackling that. Do you have enough time for coffee?"

How was that for subtle?

Renzo took a deep breath, raked a hand through his damp hair before turning the TV off and dropping the controls on the sofa. "Hell yeah, I'm having coffee. That ought to provide you with enough time to tell me what gives this morning."

He stalked into the small kitchen and flattened his tanned, calloused hands across the cracked laminate countertop a mere foot from where she poured water into the coffeepot.

It occurred to her that even now, at his most confrontational and in her face, towering Renzo Cesare and all his he-man bluster didn't intimidate her the way reedy, scrupulously mannered Miles had at the museum. Instinctively she knew Renzo could curse and stomp all day and he wouldn't scare her the way the smarmy art director had with his endless innuendo and furtive looks.

"What gives?" She measured out extra grounds to account for her guest. Her sleepover lover who seemed to be elbowing his way into her life too much, too soon. "I'll tell you what gives. I have zero experience in the morning-after department and I'm afraid of making the wrong impression."

Pressing start on the machine, she turned to face him, knowing she'd never find her inner strength or financial independence if she didn't confront obstacles head-on.

Though she had to admit, the sexy stud leaning one hip on her counter ranked as a very enticing obstacle.

He nodded slowly, his gaze fixed on the bubbling brew in the coffeemaker for a long moment. "Maybe you ought to go so far as to spell out the right impression for me. That way I can be sure I understand."

Licking her lips, she hesitated. After what had happened between them last night, how could she ever downshift their fast-moving relationship into more professional terrain?

"I just need to put the reins on things a little." She would be honest. Show her hand and see what happened. "I'm coming out of an awkward situation with a guy where I didn't stand up for myself enough and—"

"What?" Renzo tensed, hands clenching at his side. His shouted question bounced around her small kitchen in a disquieting echo. "Did someone give you a hard time? Jesus, Esme, you should have—"

"Wait!" She found herself shouting just to thwart his wild imaginings. The last thing she needed was Renzo going into Rambo mode on her creepy former employer.

Though she had to admit the image gave her a momentary smile.

"That's all in the past." Except for the bad dreams she'd had every night but the one where Renzo had occupied her bed. "It all happened weeks ago."

"What happened weeks ago?" His voice contained an ill-concealed growl that suggested he hadn't fully leashed his inner Rambo.

"I had a run-in with a guy who didn't understand the meaning of *no*. I got away from him before things turned too ugly and I've put the incident behind me." Not wishing to share too many details for fear of Renzo taking matters into his own hands, she remained vague. "But if I'm ever going to make peace with myself for what happened, I need to seek out my own strength, exercise a little more control in my life."

It was more than she'd told anyone about the situation. As the scent of coffee steamed into the air around them, Esme experienced a small catharsis. Even confiding her vow to find some more gumption had empowered her. Made her feel all the more committed to the cause.

"You need more control over your life." Renzo nodded slowly, his fist gently pounding the counter in a slow, rhythmic motion. "And you shared this with me because you want to give me the right impression."

The pounding stopped as she poured coffee into two blue ceramic mugs for them.

She shrugged as she handed him his cup. "I guess."

"You don't think I share a single damn thing in common with some perv who pushed you too far, do you, Esme? Because I swear—"

"Of course not. You are nothing like him and I know you would never…" She brushed away memories of her supervisor's unwanted advances and suffocating grip. "I know you're not like that."

His stance eased a fraction, his dark eyes shifting from sympathetic outrage to something softer, more compassionate.

"So you want me to back off because you're…" He waved his free hand in a vague motion while he juggled his steaming coffee mug in the other. "…searching for yourself?"

With great effort she prevented herself from rolling her eyes.

"I'm regrouping and finding ways to take charge of my life. Going into business for myself is actually go-

ing to give me a boost in that department and I have
you to thank for the idea. But as for a relationship..."

How could she phrase this delicately?

"A cocky construction worker commandeering
your television set isn't exactly what you had in mind,
I take it?" He set his half-empty mug on the kitchen
counter and scooped up the keys to his truck he must
have laid there the night before or this morning while
he'd been roaming around her apartment. "Heard
and understood."

Startled that he would walk away so quickly, without even arguing the point, Esme hoped she hadn't in-
advertently offended him.

Hurt him.

She hadn't really considered that possibility with a
man so supremely self-assured.

Unsure how to fix things, she shifted to the safe terrain of business discussion. "I've got a few antique clients I can start calling today. I'll let you know what
kind of reaction I get."

Renzo nodded as he moved toward the door and
Esme squelched the urge to fling herself around him
one more time and drag him back to her bedroom.
How would she ever find that core strength she
needed if she let Renzo into her life on all levels? With
her mild personality and his in-your-face arrogance,
he would all but obliterate her in no time. Wouldn't
he?

"Sounds good." He nodded. Flashed a thumbs up.
Opened her front door. "And Esme?"

"Yes?" Setting her mug down on the counter, she took a hesitant step into the living room, closer to the door. Closer to him.

"Sorry about the TV." He canted forward, his darkly handsome face blank of expression as he kissed her cheek with none of the passion that had been wrapped up in his kisses last night. "Thanks for a great time."

Before she could decide how to respond to that rather inane blow-off, the door was closed and he was gone. Leaving her much more bereft than she'd ever expected.

All because he'd given her the space she requested.

Her first awkward morning after was officially at a close and she couldn't decide how she had fared.

Had it been a success because she'd eased out of his expectations and put things back on more comfortable footing? Or had it been a miserable failure because, bottom line, she'd just sent away the hottest man on South Beach?

Frustrated, confused and more than a little depressed, Esme picked up the telephone to consult the wisdom of one of her few friends in the area. The woman whose nephew she'd accidentally stood up two nights ago.

Her new neighbor, Pauline Wolcott.

SLIDING INTO HIS TRUCK CAB, Renzo told himself he wouldn't think about the situation with Esme or the way she'd booted him out again this morning.

But as he arrived back at his house, stomping and grumbling his way from the carport to the front door, he knew he'd failed miserably at putting her out of his mind.

Charged memories from the night before played over and over. The scent of her long hair draped over them like a curtain. The disbelief mingled with plea-sure in her wide blue eyes that first time she'd come undone for him. The way she'd gone to sleep last night holding him in a grip so tight he couldn't have possibly rolled over.

Did she even remember that? Did she know her body reflexively wanted him while she was half asleep even though her damn "geeky and grateful" self didn't seem to remember when she awoke? Maybe her T-shirt declaring as much simply meant the woman was too smart for her own good.

Tromping outside through the back door of the sprawling house, he headed toward the detached workshop he'd built for his cabinetmaking business. It looked like a big gardening shed from the outside and he never brought clients here, so it's not like he broke any zoning laws. If his oldest brother ever returned from his extended stint overseas on the racing circuit, Renzo planned to buy a place somewhere a little more remote. Not that he wanted to sit by himself in the Ev-erglades, but even twenty minutes north of Miami he could find something more secluded.

Damned if he didn't find himself thinking Esme

was the kind of woman who would love to isolate herself like that.

As if.

He snorted, pissed that he kept thinking about her when he knew damn well she wasn't thinking about him today. Outside his work area, he selected a mammoth slab of maple wood that had been delivered two months ago and he hadn't found the right project for yet. Examining the piece for flaws as he sought any distinguishing characteristics of the piece, he effectively shut out thoughts of Esme for a few seconds.

And found his palms sweating at the idea of some pervert from her past manhandling her.

Reflexively, he reached for the phone in his back pocket at the same time he grabbed a fresh sheet of sandpaper and started to smooth the surface of the flawless maple slab.

"Hello?"

The sleepy feminine voice on the other end of the phone lacked the soft gentility of the woman he'd been thinking about.

"Giselle, what do I do to assure a woman I'm not an overbearing creep?"

His sister sighed through the receiver. "For starters, don't ever call her at the crack of dawn and launch into stupid questions without even saying hello."

"It's almost noon." His hand flew over the surface of the wood, sawdust flying as he balanced the cell phone against his ear. "And since when do I consult you for advice on women? These are extenuating circumstances. Cut me some slack here."

"First of all, noon is the crack of dawn when you work until 4:00 a.m. But you're not a creep. Any woman who can't tell that within the first ten minutes of talking to you is blind. But the overbearing thing... That could be a bit more of an obstacle."

Mulling that over, an idea struck as the distinctive scent of sawdust permeated the air. "You think I should introduce her to the guys who work on the construction crew? Next to them I'll look practically laid-back."

"Sure. If she sticks around a dozen testosterone-oozing males long enough to find out. Why don't you just try listening more and talking less? I think sometimes we all forget how much we ramble on at the mouth because we're used to talking right over each other. I think it freaks out the quiet types."

He could keep his mouth shut more around Esme. But somehow that didn't seem like enough.

"I just don't want her to think I'm some kind of over-possessive jerk. I'm only protective if there's a good reason."

"News flash, Ren. You find a lot more reasons than most guys. Maybe you could just take a chill pill and let this woman fight her own battles. And if you manage to do that for her, can you try and swing it for me while you're at it?"

"Great. Gang up on me why don't you?" Damn, but Giselle cut to the chase faster than his hand flying over the heavy plank in front of him. Grumbling to his sister for a few more minutes, he finished up his phone call and wondered if she had a point.

How the hell could he show Esme he wasn't overbearing if he really *was?* He wanted to help her fight her battles, damn it, not fight them for her.

His hands smoothed over the wood while he brooded. Until a light bulb flicked on somewhere inside his Cro-Magnon brain. He still didn't have any idea how to put Esme at ease.

But he suddenly knew exactly what to do with this flawless slab of maple wood.

9

ESME HAD JUST BARELY found time to change her clothes and boil water for tea when her doorbell rang. Smoothing a flustered hand over the hair she'd only just taken out of its ponytail, she flung open the door to greet her guest.

Dressed in a brilliant emerald suit featuring long silk shorts instead of pants, Pauline Wolcott looked like a walking department-store advertisement with her perfectly matched shoes and handbag, her thick gold chain around her neck.

"Good afternoon, Esmerelda." Mrs. Wolcott never failed to greet her with a formal politeness Esme's mother would appreciate. But while Pauline Wolcott was making an effort to loosen up a bit in her later years, Esme's mother still maintained the quiet aloofness and solitude that had always felt comfortable for a lifelong research librarian.

Esme invited her in and settled her on the sofa before retrieving a chipped floral teapot and the same blue ceramic mugs she'd used to serve Renzo coffee in that morning. Renzo.

Why did the thought of the man inspire the peculiar urge to emit a dreamy sigh?

"I hope you'll excuse the mugs." Esme settled the cups on a black lacquer Chinese tray she'd unearthed from the back of her cupboard and brought the drinks into the living room. "They don't give quite the same effect as your lovely silver tea service."

Tea was an event in Pauline's apartment. In fact, it had been over a cup of Earl Gray that Esme had let herself be talked into the ill-fated blind date.

Though, considering she'd met Renzo that night, perhaps it had not been so ill-fated after all.

"According to my daughter, I've wasted entirely too much of my life on ceremonial sipping and conversation anyway. Perhaps one day my silver service will be an old relic in that museum of yours." She tasted her steaming drink, a hand full of heavy dinner rings clinking against the ceramic. "But that is neither here nor there when we have more important things to discuss. Such as that enticing young man I spied leaving your apartment this morning."

Esme gulped her Darjeeling too fast, choking and sputtering at the unexpected comment.

"About the man." Where to start explaining her adventures in Club Paradise? "I stumbled across him, um—rather accidentally the other night when I was supposed to have met Hugh. I'm so—"

"I must apologize for that mix-up, my dear." Pauline leaned forward to pat Esme's hand. "Apparently my nephew's flight back to the States was delayed and he is still detained overseas with his job. I can't imagine why he didn't let me know earlier in the day when he knew I had arranged a lovely evening for him. But he is actually only my nephew by marriage, you know. His family was never as good about communication."

Shaking her head, she seemed perplexed. Esme, on the other hand, wasn't in the least surprised Hugh Duncan had found other things to do with his Saturday night than meet a blind date arranged by an eccentric step-aunt.

Relieved that she hadn't stood up the man at all, Esme hastened to reassure her neighbor. "Things worked out just fine anyway. I think it helped to mingle with new people, pry myself from the familiarity of my comfort zone."

If she hadn't gone to Club Paradise, she probably wouldn't have found the courage to boldly embrace her new stand-up attitude. The night out had let her take a few chances, delicious risks that forced her to decide the opposite of her usually conservative choices.

"Yes, well if the brawny gentleman I saw swimming laps in the pool at sunrise was the result of your mingling, I would agree things worked out for the best." Pauline settled back against a blue-and-white silk pillow Esme had picked up at one of her many garage sale expeditions. "Come now, share some details. I need practice at girl-talk so I can work up the courage to have a chat with my daughter."

Esme knew Pauline had a rather strained relationship with her daughter Brianne who owned a share of

Club Paradise. No matter their past, Esme couldn't help but think Brianne fortunate to have a mother who cared enough about her to want a closer relationship. Pauline had sold off her Palm Beach mansion and taken up residence in a very average apartment complex to be near her daughter.

"Renzo went swimming this morning?" Her mind wandered back to his damp hair. She'd just assumed he had taken a shower.

Pauline's hand fluttered delicately against her chest. "Oh yes. It made for much more interesting entertainment than the morning news. If he were twenty years older, I would have set my cap for him in no time. I've had four husbands, Esmerelda, but not one of them was Italian. And they are frightfully handsome men, don't you think?"

Esme made a note to ask Renzo if he had any uncles who were eligible bachelors. One good matchmaking turn deserved another, after all.

"Definitely handsome." There was no denying that. "But I don't know if I'm ready to jump into a relationship when I'm only just starting to get my footing again."

"We could spend our whole lives insulating ourselves from hurt, my dear. But what good is that if you aren't actually living in the process?" Pauline glanced down at the teapot and gently flicked over the tag dangling from the tea bag, as if to read the label.

"It's not just a matter of a few risks. I've done that." For the last thirty-six hours of her life anyway. "Renzo has such a strong personality that it would be easy to let him take charge, make decisions, call the shots. But I want to be in charge of me for a while and I don't want to be stuck struggling with an obstinate male to make my voice heard.''

How could she find her own strength when a muscle-bound male kept lending his? ''Is the tea hideous, by the way?''

Pauline's cheeks colored as she released the tag of the tea bag.

''No, actually it's delicious. I was just debating throwing away my tea ball in favor of these handy little bags. I think Brianne would be proud of me.'' She eased back into the sofa, her perfect posture a constant when most people would be slouching. ''And I hope you'll forgive the comparison, but I can't help but think my decades-long devotion to my silver tea service isn't all that different from your tight grip on your old habits. Maybe we both should be more adventurous.''

Much as Esme enjoyed Mrs. Wolcott's company, she couldn't deny a twinge of fear at a sudden vision of herself twenty years from now with only her books and teacups to keep her company. ''I don't mind the comparison particularly, but if I'm going to be adventurous by putting myself on the line with Renzo, you can't limit your adventures to trying out prepackaged tea bags. I think you should invite your daughter over to see your new apartment.''

Esme knew how much Pauline craved her daughter's approval. Affection.

Her neighbor bit her lip. "And if I do, you'll make another date with the sexy Italian?"

And sign on for another night of orgasmic bliss? Sure, it sounded simple.

Until Mr. Take Charge started reorganizing her life. Demanding to fight her battles for her.

Damn it, didn't she know how sorely tempted she'd been to drive him over to the museum and let him pound the living daylights out of her smarmy former employer? But any momentary satisfaction she might have gained quickly would be erased by regret that she hadn't found a way to mete out her own vengeance.

Still, Pauline blinked her mascara-laden eyes so darn hopefully that Esme didn't have a choice. Lifting her ceramic mug she proposed a toast.

"Then let's drink to it. Scaredy cats of Miami Beach unite. Here's to risk."

"And Italian men," Pauline added, a wicked gleam in her gaze.

No matter that she worried about getting tangled up with Renzo again, Esme had to drink to that one.

RENZO CHUGGED the rest of his lemonade as he slid his truck into a parking spot outside the sprawling Vizcaya arts complex a week later.

Esme had evaded him in the days following their night together, but in the middle of the week she'd asked him to meet her and a potential client at the Italian Renaissance-style villa that now served as a museum of European decorative arts.

He'd been to Vizcaya a few times to soak up the atmosphere since the place overflowed with the best turn-of-the-century furnishings from all over the world. But today's visit would be business—a chance for him and Esme to close their first significant deal as partners.

The salty breeze blew in off the bay as he straightened a rarely worn necktie and locked his truck before seeking out the place Esme had suggested they meet. Fall in Florida meant even more perfect weather than usual, the air lacking the humidity of summer while maintaining continual sunlight.

The museum and surrounding elaborate gardens had attracted moderate crowds today, but they would be thinning out soon as the dinner hour approached. Esme had assured him they would be able to remain on the property after closing if need be, as she had forged a strong relationship with one of the estate managers during her stint as an assistant museum director in South Beach.

As he reached the building he finally spied her standing near the west facade of the imposing structure where an open loggia stood flanked by two small towers. Most of the touring visitors were on the east side of the house at this time of day, leaving the forecourt of the building relatively quiet.

Leaving him and Esme almost alone.

She raised her hand to signal him over, her long floaty skirt covered with purple Indian prints and simple cotton blouse looking much more at home in this turn-of-the-century haven than her fluttery dress had in the Club Paradise disco lounge. Her blond hair was swept to one side and tied in a floppy purple ribbon, Esme's subtle sensuality was cloaked in feminine elegance and grace rather than in-your-face attitude.

A quality he couldn't help but admire.

"I've left us with a few minutes to talk before our potential client arrives." She jumped into business without preliminaries. Another cue for him to give her some room? "We're going to meet him in the casino building at the far end of the gardens, so maybe we can walk that way while we get up to speed?"

Nodding, Renzo reached behind her to urge her to lead the way and then caught himself at the last minute. He wouldn't be accused of too much touching damn it. He'd just have to ignore his natural inclinations and subvert the manners his father had drummed into his skull at an early age.

"Sounds good." He jammed his hands in his trouser pockets until the urge to touch her passed. Although, at that rate, he could be confining himself to pocket shackles all day. "Just let me know how you see my role today with this guy."

And while she was at it, wouldn't it be damn helpful if she could explain how she saw his role in her personal life, too?

Her footsteps clicked along the paved walkway,

two for his every one. Her low-key vanilla scent wafted lightly on the breeze blowing in off the bay.

"Just help me sell the guy on your work. He is a well-known society leader and he throws a lot of parties whose guest lists include all of our target clientele. If we can convince him to buy, I'm certain a lot of other locals would get in line to deal with us."

"Believe me, I won't miss an opportunity to close the deal. My brother is up at Harvard with no wheels since his car died two weeks ago. If we can't drum up some cash flow in the next few days I'm going to have to figure out another way to finance a new vehicle. It's not safe for him to be up there alone with no transportation."

The situation had been bugging him all week. He had to come up with a car for Marco soon. What if his brother needed to get to the doctor's office in a hurry? "Are you happy with your car, by the way? I'm not even sure what to purchase."

She dropped her pen on the pavement as they walked down a tree-lined lane toward the stairway that would lead to the casino—a building that looked like a small house overlooking the water and provided a focal point for the gardens.

Stooping to retrieve the pen for her, he figured a guy could at least still pick up a damn pen for a woman without being accused of chauvinism.

He tossed it up in the air and watched it turn end over end a couple of times before giving it back to her. Only then did he notice her hesitant expression.

"Don't tell me you think it's overbearing of me to recover a lost writing instrument, Esme. I thought for sure stuff like that was no big deal."

She blinked, tilted her head to one side as if she had no clue what he was talking about. "Thanks for the pen. And no, it's not a big deal. I was just thinking about your car question."

Thank you, God. He was simply being paranoid. "Got any ideas?"

"Actually, no. I happen to be between vehicles right now." She continued to plow ahead toward the stone steps leading up to the small house where they were to meet their client.

Renzo paused, thinking he must have misheard her. "Between vehicles?"

She halted, her long skirt swirling around her ankles with the arrested momentum. "Precisely. Should we press on so we can make sure we don't miss our guest?"

"Then how are you getting around town?" He thought it would be difficult for his brother to be on a self-sufficient college campus without a car? How in the hell would Esme even begin to negotiate a sprawling city like Miami without a comprehensive transit system?

She shoved up the sleeve of her white blouse impatiently. "I am acquainting myself with the bus. Not that it's really any business of yours."

"The bus?" He squelched the urge to grab his chest, but holy freaking hell didn't she realize the dangers of riding the bus around town by herself? Especially at night. "Do you know what kind of crimes can take place on a bus, let alone at a bus stop?"

"Wait. Just hold up right there." She held up her hand like she was playing crossing guard. "I've got a purse full of protective devices to ensure my safety and I really don't need a lecture on this. Can we please stick to business today?"

He didn't miss the warning in her tone. Nope. She was coming through loud and clear. Too bad his concern for her safety overrode any need to play by her rules.

"We'll get you a company car and write it off as a business expense. You're going to need it to meet with clients and—"

"Not if we meet with clients here," she argued, her blue eyes narrowing. "Vizcaya will put people in the mood to buy antiques anyway. Down the road, I'll be able to buy back my car as soon as we are assured of some income. Now, will you hurry up before we're late?"

Actually, he would make damn sure she had a car sooner than that, but he couldn't see getting her any more riled before their meeting.

A nerve twitched and pinched in his shoulders. A pain with Esmerelda Giles written all over it.

"Fine. But I hope you know I'm driving you home tonight."

TWO HOURS LATER, with the victory of closing her first true business deal pumping adrenaline through her veins like a drug, Esme would have been ready to celebrate if not for Renzo's pronouncement hanging over her.

I hope you know I'm driving you home.

His promise teased her senses even as she sat beside him in the open loggia of the casino building and watched their first-ever client walk away.

The sun had long ago set but the elaborate gardens were still visible thanks to a sprinkling of spotlights situated among the fountains and greenery for an enchanted effect.

"Congratulations, Esme." Renzo's voice wafted on the mild night breeze. "We landed our first contract thanks to you."

She couldn't have chased the smile from her face if she tried. "But we'll only be able to fulfill it thanks to you. Are you sure you can create that sideboard he wants so fast?"

"Not a problem. Thanks for steering him toward mostly premade items. We'll be paid a lot faster that way." He scooped up her paperwork and the signed contract committing the client to eight antique reproduction pieces. "And you'll get a company car right away."

Bristling, she closed her eyes. Exhaled.

"I'll buy a car very soon. I could have kept my old car for a couple more months, but I wanted to be sure I could pay my rent in between jobs. Now that we seem to have a viable business on our hands, I'll feel more comfortable making payments again."

"You've already got it all figured out, don't you?" Renzo stared out over the lush green classical gardens carved out of the subtropical terrain, then turned to meet her gaze. "Sorry if I sounded pushy about the whole transportation issue. I just couldn't afford to lose you to a bussing mishap now that my financial future is tied up in you."

The half smile he gave her sent a tiny shiver through her in spite of the temperate night air. And she had to admit his apology went a long way toward soothing her ruffled feathers.

"Then I promise to protect your investment. Should we go?" Her edgy nerves had forced the words from her mouth even though she wasn't certain she wanted to leave the timeless beauty of Vizcaya, the site of her first big business deal.

Her proximity to Renzo and the blatant sex appeal he exuded in his pinstripe suit and tie was making her forget her other mission for tonight. She needed to uphold her half of the bargain with Pauline Wolcott by spending some more time with the dark, seductive man beside her.

As they trekked out of the casino building and down the stairway toward the gardens once again, Renzo offered her his arm.

A simple, chivalrous gesture.

Except that it felt more like foreplay as she slid her hand around the solid strength of his forearm encased in the pressed silk of his jacket. She was close enough to inhale a hint of his musky aftershave, to absorb the heat of his body through two layers of shirt and jacket.

The damp fragrances of lush garden greenery, running fountains and nearby Biscayne Bay surrounded them, intensified now that night had fallen and the grounds had emptied but for them. The sultry air and moody lighting seemed to beg for a romantic encounter.

And it didn't hurt that the adrenaline of her business coup still flowed through her, providing her with restless energy and a delicious confidence she hadn't felt in far too long.

Her short heels clicked along the stone steps, echoing in time with Renzo's heavier footfall. The sound mingled with the gentle gurgle of water flowing down the water stairway beside them.

"Have you been here before?" she asked, filled with reverence to be wandering through this Italian Renaissance dreamland on the arm of a man who could have blended in on the streets of the Medicis' Florence as easily as he navigated Miami in his pickup.

She'd be a total twit if she didn't scavenge a few moments in his arms while they lingered in this classical paradise.

Alone.

"A few times. But I only bothered to take note of the furniture in the past. The gardens are all new to me." He ran his hand along a limestone wall lining the wide stairway. "Pretty cool."

"I've had a chance to grow well acquainted with the gardens." Her museum work had brought her to Vizcaya on numerous occasions. "You ought to see at least one of the grottos before we go."

Reaching the bottom of the steps that emptied out around a pool with a spewing fountain in the middle, Esme slowed her step. Her heart jumping in time with her own daring, she tugged him into one of the archways in the limestone wall leading to a private, darkened grotto.

A haven for a woman with romance on her mind.

Or more.

And without bothering to consult her partner's opinion, Esme slid her arms around him and slanted her mouth across his.

10

IN THE LOGICAL PART of his brain, Renzo wanted to be politically correct about this kiss. He really did.

Too bad his instinctive side was already caught up in the soft flame of Esme's embrace and the unmistakable message of her lips planted against his. He spoke this language fluently, damn it, and with her understated vanilla scent filling his nostrils and her slender body filling his arms, how could he interpret the signs as anything but a blinking neon green light?

She pressed closer to him in the inky darkness of the cool grotto, her slight weight backing him into a coarsely textured, bumpy stone wall behind him. Steadying himself against the solid rock he reached for her, slid his hands under her warm, long hair and smoothed them down her spine. Her fingers flexed against his chest, clutching at the lapels of his silk jacket as if to draw herself still closer.

Breaking away from the liquid fire of her kiss, Renzo sought confirmation of his interpretation. Needed her to make the call tonight since she had pushed him away last time.

"What is it you want, Esmerelda?" He lingered over the wealth of syllables in her full name, momentarily indulging the fluid accent of the Italian language all of his siblings had been forced to learn. "I need to be sure."

Her breath mingled with his in the close atmosphere of their private retreat. She met his eyes in the dim interior of the cavern that contained a stone bench and small fountain. Enough light filtered in through the archway that he could see her expression, know the heat of her gaze.

"I want the kind of pleasures you gave me the other night," she whispered, her voice so soft he almost doubted he'd heard it, except that there could be no mistaking the immediate reaction of his body, the automatic spike of the temperature between them.

"You liked the way I touched you?" He knew exactly what she meant, exactly what she wanted. Still, the idea of hearing her spell it out for him made his every nerve ending strain toward her, his erection nudging hard against his fly.

He trailed a hand down her hip, stretched his fingers across her thigh to cover as much terrain as possible. His thumb pressed into the soft flesh, eliciting a throaty hum from the back of Esme's throat.

"Yes. I liked it too much." She swayed on her feet, anchored herself to him by tucking her fingers into the waist of his trousers and hanging on tight.

Her knuckles grazed the hardened length of him, causing him to suck in an extra breath, to squeeze his eyes shut until he willed himself back under control.

"There's no such thing as liking it too much." Of that, he was damn certain.

He sought out the stone bench tucked into a far corner of the small space and scooped Esme up into his arms. "I wouldn't dream of denying you what you want."

She made a little yelp as he lifted her, yet her arms slid around his neck as easily as if they were meant to be there.

"Here?" She clutched him more tightly as he lowered himself onto the bench, settling Esme across his lap, her hip tucked snugly against the taut length of his much-taxed zipper.

"Right here," he breathed the words into the soft skin of her neck as he bent to taste her. His tongue flicked over the throbbing pulse at her throat, savoring the sweet, clean flavor of her. "Right now."

Despite the shiver that trembled through her at his words, she relaxed into his chest, her head tilted to his shoulder as her eyelids fluttered closed.

He could only see her in shades of shadow in the darkened grotto, but he knew by her parted lips and shallow breaths that her cheeks would be flushed pink by now, her full lips even more rosy than normal. He unfastened the top two buttons on her white blouse, wondering if the tight crests of her soft breasts would be suffused with that same high color. Her breathing echoed raggedly in their private outdoor chamber, the noise bouncing from one stone wall to another as the sounds of rustled clothing and throaty sighs intensified.

Baring her shoulder, he made sure to uncover only the side of her body that rested against him. If any night watchman or security person were to stumble across their hidden retreat, Esme wouldn't be exposed to their view.

Only to *his*.

Slipping his hand into the scented warmth of the hollow between her breasts, Renzo lowered his mouth to the delicate curves lifted high by the white lace bra she wore.

Her head fell back, the decadent arch of her spine lifting one dark nipple just high enough to be visible above the white lace. Falling upon that delicate flesh like a starving man, his tongue swept beneath the fabric, savoring the tight pucker of her skin against his lips.

Esme cried out, her fingers spearing their way into his hair, curving about his neck to hold him against her. A fevered need for her pulsed through his veins, a hunger to possess her now while she was so very willing.

And so very hot.

Shifting her hips on his lap, he relished the mixture of pleasure and pain her every movement wrought. He wanted to give her the fulfillment she sought, or at least that orgasm that seemed to have eluded her before him.

Damn but it felt good to know he could do that for her when no other man had succeeded.

"You're a bold man to touch me this way in a public place," she whispered in his ear, her voice breathy and ragged. "Do you think you can be a little more daring and touch me...in other places?"

"Lucky for you, *bold* has never really been a problem for me." Skimming his palm down her side, he molded the curve of her waist and hugged the swell of her hip. Reaching, trailing lower, he found the hem of her ankle-grazing skirt and allowed his fingers to burrow beneath the silky material and the satiny slip that accompanied it.

Her skin was even softer, smoother than the slippery cloth, her thighs growing warmer with every inch he ascended.

When he finally reached the barrier of white lace that separated his fingers from their goal, Esme let out a sob of mingled pleasure and frustration. Damning political correctness, Renzo bunched the fragile fabric in his palm and yanked, ripping the material off her hips in one satisfying tear.

With a cry of pleasure, she rained fierce, hot kisses across his cheek, lingered on his neck. "I'm beginning to think maybe there are benefits to an audacious man."

Pocketing the lace in his jacket, he wasted no time returning to the warmth between her thighs, always making sure her skirt covered them. He stroked his way through the silky curls shielding her sex and skimmed her slick folds.

Capturing her cry with his mouth, he kissed her, drew her lower lip into his mouth to nip and suckle. Her hips arched into his hand, seeking more of his touch.

He leaned back into the seashell-encrusted wall behind him, his jacket providing enough protection for his shoulders as he tipped Esme back with him. Their mouths sealed in a sultry tangle of tongues, he slid his finger deep inside her to savor her luscious heat.

With patience born of an absolute focus on pleasing her, Renzo ignored the sweet torment of her hip pressed and wriggling against his erection. He withdrew his finger to tease the tight bud throbbing at her center, drawing deliberate circles around that most sensitive of flesh. Replicating that movement with his tongue, he could sense her restless need, felt the tautness in her whole body.

The next time he slid two fingers inside her and she arched wildly with the impact, her thighs clenching around his hand as her body contracted in sweet spasm.

Esme clawed at his jacket even as she slumped more deeply into him.

Satisfaction resonated through him, fulfilling him even if he couldn't take her here in the shadowed grotto on Vizcaya's sprawling grounds. At least he'd been able to give her what she wanted, propelling her to the sensual heights that seemed all new to her.

He tipped his head back against the bumpy shell wall behind them, praying for enough restraint so that he could walk out of this place without too much discomfort. Yet even as he willed his breathing back to normal, Esme reached for his belt buckle and tugged on the leather strap.

Urging her fumbling fingers on, Esme absorbed the feel of cool metal against her fingertips as she unfastened Renzo's belt.

Tiny frissons of pleasure still tingled through her body, her pulse pounding between her thighs with an intensity she'd never known. She needed Renzo inside her. Now.

"Are you sure about this?" His voice whispered through the sensual haze surrounding her, penetrating her concentrated efforts to free him.

"Yes. Please. Help me." She needed him so badly her hands shook with it. Somehow what had started off as a ploy to indulge in a few stolen kisses in the most romantic setting imaginable had escalated into an erotic encounter she would remember for the rest of her life.

Her hunger for Renzo went beyond any ridiculous promise to Pauline Wolcott that she would be more adventurous. Esme wanted him with a single-minded fierceness that stunned her.

With the mixture of gentlemanly deference and absolute masculine arrogance she had come to identify as signature Renzo Cesare, he obliged her request with lightning speed. His fingers flew over the buckle and down the zipper, exposing himself to her gaze wearing nothing but silk boxers that seemed to be decorated like—

"The Italian flag?" A smile hitched at her swollen lips.

"Gotta show my pride," he managed to murmur, the words strangled as she laid her palm against his rigid length.

"You should definitely be proud," she crooned in his ear, sliding her fingers beneath the silk to wrap her hand around him. "This is a very impressive salute."

He sucked in a gasp as she skimmed a touch down his shaft.

And just as she'd hoped, he promptly ditched all talk of restraint.

Shifting her in his lap, he lifted her until she straddled him, her skirt covering their legs and concealing their intimate position beneath miles of gauzy fabric. Her sex nestled up to his, causing a delicious pressure, inciting a renewed ache.

She would have given him the condom she had in her purse if he hadn't produced one from an interior pocket of his jacket. He tore through the packaging and rolled on the device with a speed and agility that surprised her. Pleased her.

Within seconds he lifted her against him, his strong arms stretching the fabric of his sleeves until the silk lay taut against his biceps. Esme closed her eyes, focusing on the teasing proximity of his body as he positioned her right—

There.

He slid into her in one motion, filling her so completely she couldn't move, couldn't think. Could only feel him deep inside her.

He nudged her thighs a little farther apart with his hands, worked himself in by another millimeter. Just enough to hit the wall of her womb, to send a provocative shudder all the way through her.

And then he moved, lifting her up again so that he could withdraw by inches, lowering her back down again so she could feel the full import of his body inside hers.

Despite the orgasm that had pounded through her earlier, Esme found herself restless all over again, the insidious movement between her thighs calling up renewed sensual heat. As if he'd read her mind, Renzo reached between them, plucked the swollen heat of her between his clever fingers to tease and torment her.

Esme gave herself over to his control, admitting that she didn't mind Renzo's supreme self-confidence when it came to this. Another day she could take charge. Right now, she wanted to follow where he led, to see where his delicious expertise would lead them.

The unbearable tightness coiled in her belly again, the aching need he could fulfill if only he'd—

He plunged into her again, his fingers never relinquishing the pressure on her heated center.

Esme flew apart with that one sharp thrust, the tiny contractions racking her body on the inside while every nerve ending went berserk on the outside. She rode the waves of pleasure, her hips grinding against his in unconscious rhythm until he howled with his own release, his fingers sinking into the soft flesh of her hips with primal ownership. He drew her tightly to him, sealing their bodies in a carnal union of pleasure, the sultry night air wrapping around them like a lover's whisper.

Her head reeled, her body throbbed with the resonating pleasure. The scent of sex swirled around them, mingling with the mossy green fragrance that permeated the grotto.

Replete, she didn't think she could move, let alone speak. And as much as she had enjoyed their unconventional location for a tryst, a part of her wished they were tucked safely in her bed where she could fall asleep in his arms.

Although that same scenario had unsettled her a week ago, Esme had since been able to glimpse a professional future for herself as an antiques broker and the experience had given her more confidence. Even a little daring, maybe.

No more would she be a woman to be trifled with, and Renzo seemed to have already adjusted his dealings with her to take that into account. She had a feeling he wouldn't be so quick to rearrange her life or her electronics equipment if they were to spend the night together again.

Maybe the time had come to take another chance.

LONG FEMININE SILENCES meant big thinking for women like Esme.

While Renzo would have preferred to believe she

lay against his chest simply reveling in the afterglow of sizzling sex, he knew her well enough to know that if she hadn't moved yet, she was probably thinking big thoughts.

Like how to toss him out of the grotto without losing his business partnership.

At least, the last time they'd shared an intimate encounter, that had been the outcome. Esme had lain in her bed thinking about how to sidle out of the sensual terrain and put them back on professional footing.

This time, he'd spare her the trouble. Show her he was willing to play by her rules until she worked out whatever issues she had with overbearing males. Or—God forbid—until he figured out a way to be a little less overbearing himself.

Damn.

Scrambling for the right way to cool things down before she could accuse him of taking control, Renzo tilted his head to lean back against the textured expanse of the shell-lined wall behind him.

How did one give space to a woman who had made it clear she wasn't ready for a relationship? A woman who was struggling with how to assert herself in life?

"What do you say we head to the lawyer's office tomorrow and we can legitimize the partnership? Tie up all the loose ends, make sure things are legally binding?" How was that for cool-as-you-please? She couldn't accuse him of trying to take control after lovemaking this time. Not when he was so clearly offering to put legal assurances of their professional equality in her hands.

Yet, the grotto remained eerily silent in the aftermath of his question. Esme unnaturally still.

"Esme?" He gripped her shoulders, her head tucked under his chin. "What do you think?"

Straightening, she met his gaze, her expression difficult to gauge through the heavy shadows, but her cool tone abundantly clear. "Sounds like a very reasonable plan. Shall we go?"

She slid off his lap, busying herself with righting her clothes and smoothing her long hair.

"I said the wrong thing again, didn't I?" What the hell made him think he could have any kind of relationship with a quiet woman? How did a guy know what these quiet types were thinking?

Then again, since when was he even interested in a relationship?

Hadn't he sworn off women since Celeste? At least, he had until Esme. The significance of Esmerelda being the first woman he'd slept with since then suddenly seemed to multiply. Quiet or not, this woman had become important to him very quickly.

"Of course you didn't say the wrong thing." Esme retrieved her paperwork from their business meeting and slid her purse strap over her shoulder again. "It's just that I'm accustomed to having all my clothes back in place before wading through business conversations and talk of seeking an attorney. Sorry if I wasn't prepared for the mood shift."

Renzo tucked and zipped, all the while watching Esme's clipped movements as she obsessively straightened the edges of her stack of papers.

"Okay, sarcasm I can work with. I did a bad job with the segue, so sue me." He stepped outside the grotto, sorry to leave their quiet haven and the all too rare moment of mutual understanding behind them. "I was only trying to save you the effort of resurrecting a little distance between us. It's a peculiarity of yours—you're not exactly the post-sex cuddling type. Remember how you kicked me out of your apartment last time?"

Esme had followed him into the gardens, but her shoes stopped their clicking as he posed his question.

"I did *not* kick you out of my apartment."

"You couldn't hustle me out of there fast enough, woman. Admit it." He stepped back to nudge her forward. "I just thought I'd spare you the stress of figuring out what to do with me this time. This is no stress, okay?" He held his hands up to demonstrate. "No pressure from this guy."

Esme shook her head, resumed her step. Her long hair bounced along in time with her feet hitting the path as they walked away from the Vizcaya grounds toward the parking area. A smile softened her mouth.

"You're an intriguing man, Renzo Cesare. Care to tell me why you bother with me and my so-called peculiarities when you could have your pick of women?"

"Why I *bother* with you? Aside from the fact that you're damn fine to look at—which is actually not even a big factor for me—you've got this part conservative, part wild-woman thing going on that's sort of fun to watch. I never would have pegged you for a sex-in-the-grotto type of woman and yet you just knocked me on my ass back there. Maybe I just want to see what you do for a follow-up act."

He could go on and on about what he found attractive about her, but he doubted she would care to hear it in her effort to maintain space.

Besides, he was only just starting to realize how much he saw in her.

As they neared his truck, the lone vehicle left in the lot, Esme slowed.

"Have you had many serious relationships?" Casting him a considering look, she ran a hand over her bare arm in the cooling night air.

"One. I ended up alone at the altar though, so I take it things weren't as serious on her side. How about you?" He unlocked her side of the truck, grateful she hadn't breathed a word about taking a bus home.

Her expression softened, her brow furrowed in gentle empathy. Not what he needed from her, damn it.

He nudged her closer to the open door before she could quiz him about being ditched at the altar. "Come on, fess up. Do you have miles of broken hearts in your past, Esme?"

"Zero. This dating thing is pretty much uncharted terrain for me. I've been too buried in art history and commitment to work to date. No, I take that back. I think I've just been too chicken to date because I was never particularly good at it." She accepted his arm to lever herself up to the high running board and into the truck cab. "How long ago did your fiancée pull the disappearing act?"

"Six months ago. I swore off women until you. Being left at the altar has a way of killing the healthiest libidos. Temporarily, anyway." He grinned up at her as he tucked the long skirt closer to her body so he wouldn't close it in the door. "You ready to go?"

"Almost. You do realize I'm obvious rebound material, right?" She propped the door open with one hand so he couldn't close it. "I'm sure this is just one of those quickie-fling things and we'll move past it in no time."

She flashed him an overbright smile before letting go of the door as if to signal this discussion was closed.

Rebound material?

Renzo found himself at a strange loss for words at that statement. Esme obviously didn't know the first thing about him if she thought he jumped into any relationship just for the fling.

He might have only made it to the altar once, but that didn't mean he had ever dated lightly. His father had instilled too much respect for women into his skull to ever treat a female with anything but high regard.

And damned if Esme didn't inspire the fiercest sense of protectiveness he'd ever felt for any woman. Which—for an overbearing kind of guy—was probably a surefire sign he was well on his way to starting much more than a fling.

11

GRINDING GEARS AS SHE upshifted through five-o'clock traffic on Ponce de Leon Boulevard the following week, Esme hoped she wouldn't regret buying a used car without an automatic transmission. Watching the tachometer with one eye and the road ahead through the other, she hit third gear like an old pro and experienced a rush of frivolous pride.

She could do this.

Taking control of her own life since she'd gone into business with Renzo had been tremendously freeing. She'd managed to line up enough orders for antique reproductions that Renzo even needed to hire some extra help.

Or so he'd told her on the phone last night.

She hadn't actually seen him in person since their close encounter in the sultry grotto. Probably a good thing considering she'd waded in over her head as far as their relationship went.

Now, as she sped toward his house to go over the new product orders, Esme tried to tell herself that he'd been right to back off the other night. Although she'd been disappointed to have their night cut short, she'd realized her life was too much of a mess right now to impose on anyone else. Even though she'd had some success digging her way through the wreckage of her former existence, she still spent as much time ruminating over the past as she spent looking toward the future.

A trend she refused to continue.

She simply couldn't get involved with anyone until she confronted a few old demons. Well, really just one old demon—her touchy-feely ex-employer at the museum. In order to find some peace with all that happened, she needed to tell that man exactly what she thought of him. She needed to file complaints about him to every organization imaginable.

One thing she'd learned from her new business partnership with Renzo was that her voice deserved to be heard. And it would be.

Just as soon as she worked up a little more nerve.

Esme steered her dark-blue Ford into Renzo's driveway, grateful for the sense of peace she felt now that she'd made up her mind. Two other trucks loomed in the driveway beside Renzo's—one jet black with a short bed and shiny silver mag wheels, the other a pared-down version of Renzo's blue pickup, complete with the words Cesare Construction printed on the door in gold block lettering.

Disappointment pinched as she realized she wouldn't have Renzo all to herself. Then again, every time they got within winking distance of one another lately, they ended up ripping their clothes off, something she couldn't risk since realizing she wasn't fit for any relationship right now. Maybe the extra company parked in Renzo's driveway could prevent them from giving in to that primal urge.

Walking around to the back of the house, Esme skirted an overgrown patch of birds of paradise and a few hibiscus bushes sorely in need of tending to find the workshop in back. Rock music from at least a decade ago drifted on the wind before she caught sight of her quarry—the man she needed to convince herself to stay away from—one Renzo Cesare.

He stood on a wide canvas tarp beside two other men. All of them hunched over a stout, early American sideboard.

As her heel moved from the soft earth of the lawn to the flagstone of a small garden path right behind them, the three men turned to look at her.

Renzo moved first, switching down the silver boom box perched on the edge of the canvas. One of the other men, a lean blonde sporting a buzz cut and enough muscles for the pro wrestling circuit, set aside a rag he used to stain the sideboard. The third man who looked so much like Renzo it could only be a brother smiled broadly and took a step closer, but Renzo was at her side first. He slipped a possessive arm around her waist and drew her away from the others.

"How did you get here?" His voice softened to a pitch only the two of them would hear, yet there wasn't anything soft about the tone. "You didn't—"

"I bought a car." She dangled her new key chain

from the Ford dealership in front of his nose. "Hello to you, too." She would have greeted his friends, but his arm around her waist tightened, the warmth of his fingers spearing through the silk of her blouse.

"You bought a car?"

"Lock, stock and barrel. It was the newest used car on the lot." And the best deal ever, damn it. "Now, aren't you going to introduce me to your friends?"

The man had the manners of a pit bull. Still, she had to admit the glint of admiration in his eye helped make up for a few forgotten pleasantries.

"Okay. But then I want to go check it out myself. Did you know you're supposed to have a mechanic look at it before you buy?"

She rolled her eyes and slipped out of his grip, curious about the men working with him. Behind her, she could hear him sigh as he followed her.

She didn't need to wait long for introductions since the taller, dark-haired guy was already offering his hand, "I'm Nico Cesare, the Neanderthal's brother. Very much at your service."

"Esmerelda Giles. Nice to meet you." She shook his hand, noting on closer inspection that Nico wasn't quite a clone of his brother. His features were sharper, with a nose that looked like it had seen the wrong end of a few street fights. He topped Renzo by maybe an inch, his movements economical and efficient as opposed to his brother's lazy grace.

She had to tug her hand back from his lingering grasp, yet she sensed he touched her simply to get a reaction from Renzo. Who promptly muttered something about the egotism of professional athletes.

As with Renzo, Esme acknowledged that this man built like a linebacker could squeeze her hand and she wouldn't feel the least bit threatened, whereas her ex-employer had probably only weighed thirty pounds more than her and he'd intimidated her with just a look.

Renzo's arm materialized at her waist again before he nudged her away from Nico and closer to the buzz-cut blonde.

"And this is Brody Healy, who has much better manners than my brother. Brody's my best cabinet guy so I thought I'd see how he liked working on the reproductions."

Esme shook his hand before peering over his considerable shoulder at the cherry sideboard piece he seemed to be distressing.

"The wood looks marvelous." Pleased, she smiled up at the younger man and received a grin with an honest-to-God blush in return.

She had the feeling Brody would have fit right in with the history geeks in college. He was the kind of guy she knew how to relate to, the kind of guy who would never be too pushy or in your face.

Too bad Esme had never been overly attracted to that kind of man.

Nico snapped a bright orange hibiscus flower off a nearby stem and handed the bloom to her as he joined them. "We finished up a few other pieces that are drying inside the workshop. Would you like to see?"

Renzo butted in between them before Esme could say yes. "Easy, dawg. She promised to show me something first, so you and your belated attempts at good etiquette can just get back to work."

He steered Esme toward the gently sloping side lawn full of overgrown tropical flowers, but not before she caught Nico sending her a wink.

Renzo glowered so hard she thought he'd burst into flames.

"He's harmless, he's just hell-bent to give me a hard time." He guided her around to the front of the house, leaving Nico and Brody to their work in the backyard so he could see her new car parked in the driveway.

"See? Four perfectly safe wheels. No more buses for this independent woman." Could she help it that she lifted her chin a little at the statement? No offense to the bus—and in fact, thank God for mass transit—but still, she'd been pretty damn proud of herself to waltz into the dealership, haul out her best garage sale haggling skills, and drive away with a great car.

She wasn't surprised in the least to see Renzo already crawling under the hood, kicking tires and studying the dials across her dashboard.

When he finally came up for air, he was smiling. "Two thumbs up, lady. You snagged yourself some nice wheels."

"Bet you didn't think I could handle the car dealers, did you?" She remembered Renzo had asked to go car shopping with her every day that week. She intended to deliver a haughty sniff, but she was so damn proud of her new purchase that she ended up grinning instead. "Did I mention I bought it for a song?"

Renzo shut the car door and made his way back to her, his dark eyes locked on hers.

"I know you can handle yourself. Maybe I just thought I could help. Provide moral support, input, whatever. For that matter, I have to buy a car for my brother, too. I thought we could have used that buying power to leverage an even better deal." He shrugged. Ran restless fingers through his silky dark hair. "I know you're on this quest to prove something to yourself, Esme, but don't think for a second you have to prove anything to *me*."

His body loomed close to hers suddenly, the force of his will a palpable thing between them. She stifled a shiver, squelched the need to reach out and touch him.

"My mother taught me that if I didn't expect much in life, I'd never be disappointed." And maybe, for a research librarian who'd never gotten married, never ventured out of the neighborhood she'd grown up in, it had been an important life lesson to avoid disappointment. "But I am beginning to realize that if you don't have a few high expectations in life, if you don't strive to be the best you can be, how on earth can you ever achieve great things?"

Her mother may have been content to insulate herself from failure by not taking any risks, but Esme refused to live that way any longer.

Renzo's thick, dark eyebrows inverted in a downward slash. "I don't get it. You've already taken a huge risk by going into business for yourself, by venturing out on a blind date that turned out to be a date with a total stranger... You're taking a lot of risks already."

But she couldn't take the biggest risk yet. The risk of falling in love with a sexy, arrogant woodworker who made her knees weak just by standing close to her.

Not that she would let him know that.

"Those are all new risks I've just taken in the last few weeks. It's going to take more than that to demonstrate to myself that I don't need anyone's approval, that it's enough for me to respect who I am and what I do." She leaned back against the sun-warmed front fender of her new car. "I spent years working as an assistant to a slimeball at the museum when I was doing all his work plus mine, and yet I let him get away with treating me less than professionally for years. Why? Didn't want to rock the status quo. Besides, I'd never expected much glory or recognition as the assistant to a museum director, so why should I have been surprised when I didn't get any? I settled for second best for too long."

"The pervert who hit on you was your boss?" Renzo's volume increased with every word out of his mouth.

Oddly, his anger only comforted her. She wished she'd had the sense to be that outwardly furious with Miles Crandall when he'd hauled her into an unwanted lip lock. Instead she'd simply fought her way free and bolted, keeping her fury locked inside.

She needed to take a page from Renzo's book.

"Pretty smarmy, wasn't it? But that incident still plays havoc with me. I need to find a way to deal with that before I go forward and—" *jump your bones again. Fall head over heels for you* "—make peace with myself."

MORE LIKE THE PERV would be making peace with the asphalt beneath his nose when Renzo finished with him.

Knowing that saying as much would be counter-productive at this point, however, Renzo forced himself to remain silent.

He bit his tongue. Closed his eyes. Squeezed his temples in a pincer grip to alleviate the fury pulsing through his veins.

He would wait to kick ass at the museum until another day. Right now, he needed to let Esme know she had a hell of a lot more going for her than she realized.

And thanks to his brother's help yesterday, he had the perfect way to prove it to her.

She waved a sheaf of papers in front of his nose. "I actually brought a couple of new furniture requests for us to go over. Do you have a few minutes?"

"You got more orders?" The woman must spend far too much time working to have wrangled as many sales as she had in the past week. "Don't you ever sleep?"

"I'm too excited over the prospect of regular income

again to even think about sleeping." She hitched at the short sleeve of her silk blouse, drawing his attention to her lightly tanned arms and a jingling charm bracelet around one wrist. "Should we go inside to work on these?"

He wanted to take her inside all right. Straight to his bedroom so they could lock the door behind them and remember exactly why they were better off together than apart.

"No. I don't want to work and I don't want to go inside." He slid the papers from between her fingers and tossed them onto the front seat of her car through the open window.

"And since when is being in business for yourself a matter of doing whatever you want?" Frowning, she reached to retrieve her notes.

"Since I decided it's more important for you to make peace with yourself than it is for us to discuss new sales. I've got something I want to show you." Palming the small of her back, her propelled her forward.

Glaring over her shoulder, she dug her heels in. "Why do *you* get to decide we ignore business?"

"Because *I* went to the trouble to make you a gift that you need to see." He nudged her forward again, more gently this time. "Will you come with me? Please?"

"A gift?" Some of the starch seeped out of her shoulders, her feet moving along more amiably. "For me? But my birthday's four months away."

As he led her around the back of the house again, he managed to catch his brother's eye and give him the high sign to haul ass out of there. He wanted to be alone with Esme for this.

"It's not that kind of present." How to explain the gift he'd *had* to make for her? After he'd discovered that slab of maple wood, the thing sort of took shape of its own volition. "You'll see."

By the time they reached the canvas where Brody and Nico had just finished working, the outdoor walkway lights had flicked on in deference to the sunset. Thankfully, his mouthy helpers left without giving him a hard time, Nico only pausing long enough to snag a bank check to cover a car down payment since he planned to bring a vehicle up to Boston that weekend.

"I hope they didn't leave on our account." Esme inspected the cherry sideboard by the dim light cast from the walkway lamps.

"Nah," he lied, eager to show her the project he'd been working on all week. "They should have gone home a long time ago. Now, are you coming with me to see this thing or am I going to have to carry you?"

She blinked those wide blue eyes at him, eyes far more canny than he'd realized when they first met. "I can certainly walk." She tilted her stubborn little chin and stared down her nose at him. "Wouldn't want you to hurt yourself."

He plucked her off her feet and tossed her over his shoulder, ignoring a squeal of laughing protest. The position aligned her hip with his cheek, tempting him sorely to give her thigh a quick nip through the wheat-colored linen of her skirt.

By the time he ducked into the small wooden work shed in the backyard, the fragrance of night-blooming jasmine gave way to the tang of fresh sawdust and the lightly chemical scent of dried polyurethane. He slid Esme down to her feet, taking his time to appreciate the subtle curves of her slender body.

And damn, hadn't it been too long since he'd held her?

Their gazes locked as their thighs brushed. Only he didn't see a wary woman who avoided taking chances. The Esmerelda Giles in his eyes looked ready to wriggle her way out of her clothes and back into his arms.

Ignoring the caveman urge to drag her to his bed and keep her there for days, Renzo took a step back, determined to prove something to her.

"I've been working on this all week," he started, his voice rough with too much desire. Too much hope.

Hadn't he learned anything about not rushing into relationships after the debacle with Celeste? Clearing his throat, he fingered the drop cloth that covered his creation standing in the middle of the floor and started again.

"That is, I've been working on this in all my spare time simply because the idea possessed me once I figured out what I needed to make." He hitched up a corner of the soft cotton fabric and twisted the material between his fingers. "I found this huge piece of maple wood a while ago and—don't laugh—I thought of you as soon as I touched it."

Esme took a step closer, her charm bracelet jingling in time with her step.

Yanking away the cover, he revealed the huge Colonial-style desk with its smooth, broad surface and clean lines. The sound she made was a half gasp, half chirp, a mixture of surprise and pleasure. As she knelt in front of it, her fingers automatically reaching to smooth over the dull sheen of the antiqued finish, Renzo experienced a damned annoying catch in his chest.

A definite clench in his heart.

"That thick, stalwart maple was so solid and steadfast, it just said 'Esme' to me." And the decision to make her the desk had been that clear-cut, that simple. "It seemed like the kind of thing a woman in business for herself ought to have. I hope it reminds you how strong you really are."

12

EVEN IN THE THROES of her most glorious garage-sale finds, Esme had never experienced such an urgent need to possess an object.

The desk gleamed dully in the low light cast by the rustic sconces on the walls of the work shed. The warm red-honey tone of the maple wood was as inviting as the simple, hearty style of the Colonial piece.

And it was huge.

She felt like Alice in Wonderland next to that gargantuan piece of furniture, her hand small and insignificant against the broad surface as she reached to touch it.

"You made this for me?" She seemed to recall he'd said as much, yet she couldn't reconcile what possessed him to create such a splendid piece more suited for a high-level executive than a woman who'd been two steps away from destitution.

"I had to make it for you. I've been staring at this slab of maple for months and then once we met—" He snapped his fingers, the sound piercing the stillness of the small building. "I knew exactly what to do with it."

Esme smiled at the idea of being someone's inspiration. "I love it. It's absolutely magnificent." Her hands smoothed over the grain, absorbing the nuances of the wood. "But I can't imagine how you made the connection between me and this gorgeous piece of furniture. It's so solid. So...strong."

Behind her, she sensed his approach. Felt his step on the hardwood floor as the movement reverberated through her feet.

"That fearless determination to take on a business of your own feels pretty solid to me." His voice soothed and inflamed her senses at the same time, stirring something deep inside her.

"That wasn't fearless. That was desperation."

"Then what about all the clients you've signed on already? Is that desperation, too? Or is it unwavering dedication to the path you've set for yourself?" Renzo's hands dropped to her shoulders, his fingers flexing into the silk of her blouse.

She turned toward him, unable to swallow back a tear that threatened. His generous act packed enough punch to overwhelm her all by itself, but she was even more touched that he would see her in such a flattering light.

How could she disappoint him when he had so much faith in her?

"I don't know that I've been the poster child for self-assurance in my past, but you can bet I'm going to be inspired by this beautiful desk from now on." She gulped past the catch in her throat, drawn in by the heat in his dark brown eyes. "Thank you."

A half smile twitched his lips as his hands trailed lightly down her arms. "Would you think my present was totally self-serving if I angled for a thank-you in the form of a kiss?"

Her throat went dry. Or maybe that was simply because her heart had suddenly lodged there. She couldn't seem to find words just now, but she was only too happy to oblige.

Moving firmly into his personal space, Esme thrilled to the heat of his big body next to hers. His arms went around her, drawing her close.

And he was all about strength. Esme couldn't imagine how he saw it in her when he seemed to exude it from every pore. His limbs were all about ripped muscles and raw strength, and Esme couldn't get enough of him.

She stretched up to touch her mouth to his, to grant him that small favor he'd requested. A kiss was a simple thing, really. It shouldn't have the power to turn her knees to liquid and her resolve to ashes, yet no sooner had she angled her head to accommodate him than his lips set her on fire.

She'd told herself she needed to break free of her past first, but all thoughts of the past grew dim and faded in light of the white hot present and Renzo's slow possession of her mouth. The velvet stroke of his tongue made her eyelids fall closed, the deft touch of his hands around her waist reminded her why it was so very good to be a woman.

And to be wanted.

Vowing to set things right in her past soon, tomorrow even, Esme wrapped her arms around Renzo's neck and clung. Whatever the future held, she wouldn't find it by hanging back and waiting.

"Thank you," she whispered the words between kisses and pulled him with her as she stepped backward to the door. "I have even more gratitude to show you if you come with me."

"I don't need gratitude," Renzo growled, his footsteps shuffling along with hers as they moved outside into the warm night air. "But then again, if you're really determined…"

"I'm unwavering on this point." She tossed back his words from earlier as the scent of jasmine wound round them along with the sounds of nighttime in the neighborhood—a few kids still playing, other kids being called in for the night, the laughter of a late dinner party.

"What kind of gentleman would I be if I got in the way of a determined woman?" He looped his arms around her neck, allowed her to tug him across the yard and through the back door of the house.

"Not a very lucky one, that's for sure." Esme stalled inside the kitchen since she had no clue where the bedroom might be. She hooked a finger in the collar of his T-shirt. "You want to get lucky, partner?"

Renzo decided then and there he could gladly take an occasional back seat to the kind of woman who issued invitations like that one.

Somehow, when Esme twisted his shirt around her

finger, she twisted him right along with it. He could damn well spend a lifetime of days compromising with her if it meant he could spend a lifetime of nights just like this.

How could he mind a woman who took the lead when they ended up tangled in his sheets?

"I'm feeling damn lucky already." He molded his fingers to the curves of her hips, drawing her lower body flush against his. "It's not every day a beautiful woman shows up at my workplace and drags me to bed to have her way with me."

Esme's eyelids fluttered as she hissed in a gasp between clenched teeth. Her reaction to their hips locked together definitely didn't hurt his ego.

Of course, he hovered near hyperventilation status himself just from the soft feel of her thighs. The promise of so much more.

"Strong and beautiful all in one day?" Esme pulled him down the hall toward the bedrooms, even though she couldn't possibly know her way around the house. "You'd better be careful, or you're going to turn my head."

He paused outside of his room—it wasn't the master bedroom, but it had been his since childhood. He'd shared it with Nico long ago, but he'd far rather share it with Esme Giles tonight.

"I wouldn't want to turn your head just yet. I'm sneaking up on you, Esme. I plan to wheedle my way into your bed and into your heart before you know what hit you."

Not giving her a chance to think about that for too long, Renzo leaned in to kiss her. He wanted all her attention on the here and now anyway. The future and the past both seemed to unsettle Esme, but she definitely knew how to wrest every last bit of pleasure from the present.

She backed him into the tall Colonial rice bed that had been his first substantial furniture project the summer he turned eighteen. She seemed determined to keep a physical upper hand tonight as she shifted and maneuvered him right where she wanted him. Renzo didn't mind letting her be on top, but if he was going down, he was taking her with him.

Her grip on his shoulders tightened as he tumbled them both into the unmade tangle of blankets, keeping her anchored against him.

A slow smile spread across her face, a naughty gleam lit up her eyes.

"Then I'm sure you'll be very patient while I undress you." Already her hands slid down his thighs to tug his jeans down his hips.

Ah, hell.

He sensed imminent sensual torture on the horizon, but he couldn't exactly retract the offer now. She slid down the length of his body, backing up on all fours to pull the denim off his feet. Her breasts grazed his legs as she shifted rather deliberately over him. The soft weight stroking over him reminded him exactly how much he wanted to undress her.

But the stakes tonight were more than simple pleasure. He wanted to tear down the boundaries she seemed determined to keep in place, to prove to her that he could let her take the lead sometimes. And although that might be easier to do in bed than out of it, somehow he knew the pain of Celeste leaving him at the altar would be like a hammer on his thumb compared to the buzz-saw cut to his heart if he couldn't win over Esme.

He weathered the slow torment of her lithe body wriggling, shifting and crawling over his until she'd stripped every last piece of fabric from him. Renzo needed every ounce of self-control to keep his hands to himself. The need to touch her, to palm a thigh or skate a few fingers underneath her skirt, inundated him.

"Patience doesn't come easy for a man like me," he reminded her as she kissed her way down his chest, her lips pausing mere inches away from a raging, on-fire and sure-to-be-the-death of him erection.

Esme levered herself up to a sitting position, her fingers moving to work the buttons on her blouse. "Then maybe your efforts deserve a little recognition." She shimmied out her blouse, the movement jiggling her lace-covered breasts in a way that made his mouth water and his hands twitch to cup the soft mounds.

"You're killing me." He didn't care what kind of good intentions he'd had tonight, if he didn't touch her soon he'd lose his mind.

She stretched out on top of him, pressing sweet flesh to his burning skin. "Maybe I can help. As long as you let me stay right here, I think it would be okay if you undressed me."

"With pleasure." His hands skimmed her rib cage up to the icy-blue lace that hid her from view.

Straps off, hook unfastened and the thing was sailing across his bedroom to land on his bureau. She purred when he stroked his thumbs across the delicate points of her breasts, her back arching to give him better access. And although he couldn't wait to get inside her, to strip away every last inch of fabric covering her body, he found he had all the time in the world when it came to giving this woman what she wanted.

He drew on one taut peak and then the other, alternating the stroke of his tongue with the glide of his fingers until Esme's hips twisted against his in an insistent, notice-me rhythm.

Her vanilla scent filled his nostrils along with the musky scent of desire. He thrust both hands up her skirt, over her thighs to find the satin straps holding her lace panties in place. Careful not to be too hasty with more of her lingerie, he slid the insubstantial garment down delicious curves, shifting her legs to one side so he could ease the lace and the skirt to the floor.

Still, Esme had no intention of being unseated. After rolling on a condom, she straddled his thighs again, positioning herself directly above him.

Easing down the length of him in one silken stroke, Esme levered herself into place with her hands on his chest. The cry in her throat paled in comparison to his roar of satisfaction that resonated through the room.

He'd waited forever for this woman and the fierce heat of their connection seemed like undeniable proof they belonged together.

When she collapsed against his chest, holding herself very still as he moved inside her, he knew instinctively she was giving him the reins once again.

Curving one arm around her waist, he rolled her to her back and shifted the pillow carefully beneath her head. Eyes at half-mast, she looked up at him with smoky desire in her gaze.

He didn't have any intention of disappointing her. In fact, filled with the need to let her know they belonged together, Renzo made slow, thorough love to her. Each retreat from her tight heat urged him to come back for more and more. She met his every thrust, shivered at his every kiss until her body flushed pink, her lips trembling with that ultimate sensual need.

Withdrawing partway, he reached between them to touch the swollen heat of her. He feathered a finger across that throbbing center until her whole body went taut.

When he thrust deep inside her the next time, she unraveled on contact. Her scream filled the room, reverberating through his chest and into his heart.

Those tiny, tight pulses of her feminine muscles nudged him over the edge, his completion feeling so damn good he about blacked out from the rush of life force out his body.

When he snapped out of it, he realized he was still

lying on top of her, not nearly careful enough about not crushing her. Rolling to his side, he tucked her drowsy body into his blankets, drawing her head on his chest.

And he'd never felt so complete in his life.

Six months after Celeste had left him standing at the altar, Renzo finally figured out why he had never felt compelled to chase after her. Fate had a different woman in mind for him all along, and he didn't have any intention of letting Esmerelda Giles slip away.

THE MOMENT ESME OPENED her eyes the next morning, she knew she needed to leave.

Definitely, absolutely *had* to slip away ASAP.

Too bad she'd never been so divinely comfortable in her entire life. She lay on her side in Renzo's bed while he lay behind her, spoon-style. His arm draped over her waist, his hand flat against the mattress mere inches from her breast.

Sensual longing jolted through her even at 5:00 a.m. Even though she'd been intimate with him just two hours ago. And two hours before that, and forty-five minutes before that...

Their night together should have worn her out but instead she felt energized, ready to take on the world.

Eager to face old demons.

Sliding from the nest of warm blankets, Esme knew she needed to act now before she shifted forward just enough to put her breast in Renzo's hand. She could easily spend another hour or twenty tangling the sheets with this impossibly sexy man.

Retrieving her clothes—including the bra strewn over a framed photo of Renzo and his brother Nico in a Florida Panthers hockey uniform—she penned a quick note letting him know the time had come for her to settle an old score.

The gift Renzo had given her last night cemented her decision to embrace her future and be the woman Renzo seemed to see when he looked at her.

She wouldn't be worthy of a relationship with Renzo or the gorgeous, solid maple desk he'd made for her until she proved to herself she could be as strong as he claimed. After the way they'd made love last night—as if they'd never get enough of one another—she was more determined than ever to wave goodbye to the old, insecure Esme.

Still, in order to claim any happily-ever-after for herself, the new Esme felt the need for some old-fashioned butt kicking first.

13

OKAY, SO MAYBE she would admit the plans that seemed brilliant at 5:00 a.m. before the benefit of any coffee occasionally turned out to be the dumbest ideas in life.

Esme promised herself this was not one of those times as she pulled into the parking lot of the Southern Florida Museum building on South Beach, just down the road from Club Paradise where she and Renzo had met. Where she'd first realized she needed to stop hiding from life and start confronting it head-on.

Of course, the free champagne that night had probably helped make her a bit bolder. Just now as she stepped through the employee entrance at the back of the museum shortly after seven, Esme longed for a little more of that bravado and a lot less of the nausea roiling through her belly at the thought of confronting Miles.

Renzo could do this.

The notion appeared in her mind out of nowhere, a gentle assurance that gave her a much-needed injection of confidence. And Renzo wouldn't only confront a detractor because he was big and bad and had the power to intimidate with just the flex of his shoulders.

No, Renzo was the kind of man who would face his critics simply so he could sound off and make his opinion known. Exactly the reason Esme needed to take on Miles Crandall this morning.

She walked down the dim, well-air-conditioned corridor toward the museum offices, the same path she'd tread every morning for five years. Following an exciting postgraduate internship at the Floridian arts center, she had been thrilled to remain there after receiving her degree, quickly working her way up to the assistant director position.

Now, as she passed old photographs of the Everglades through the last century, she experienced the familiar tingle of anticipation she'd felt every day she'd traversed this corridor. Working in a museum combined the best garage sale euphoria with the assurance she could have it all at no cost. The treasures within would always be accessible to all—exquisite finds that were absolutely free for the viewing.

As she paused in front of a footprint cast of a jaguar, Esme realized her work with Renzo could never fully take the place of her museum job. As much as she loved antiques, she needed to involve herself more deeply in art history again. Once the antiques business grew a reputation, it wouldn't be hard to juggle both jobs. After all, Renzo had his construction company.

And, damn it, she owed it to herself to follow her own dreams.

If Miles Crandall thought he could intimidate her into running scared from her brass ring, he had another thing coming. Being with Renzo—seeing him have confidence in his own decisions and the courage to follow his convictions—had inspired her to live on her own terms.

Bravado in place, Esme marched past the door to her old office and smelled the coffee brewing in the small break room beside it. Ever a creature of habit, Miles took his coffee precisely at 7:30 a.m. before meeting with his staff at eight o'clock. She had the perfect window of opportunity to speak to him along with the guarantee of reinforcements nearby. He wouldn't dare mess with her when his co-workers were within shouting distance.

Because she wasn't here to make nice, Esme barged into his office without knocking.

And damn well succeeded in surprising him.

Miles held a painfully young intern in his arms, his reedy arms locked around a slender brunette in a neat blue suit. He released her rather abruptly at Esme's intrusion, sending the wide-eyed woman stumbling back a step.

"You scum-sucking sleaze." Esme could find no other words. She didn't need to ask if the trembling brunette had been a willing partner just now. She recognized too much of herself in the twenty-something's eager-to-succeed appearance and shell-shocked expression.

"Jealous, Esme?" Miles had the gall to look pleased with himself as he straightened his understated green tie and leaned a hip into his imposing cherry desk.

With an irreverence born of nerves and fury, Esme couldn't help but think her desk was much nicer. And bigger.

Behind her she heard Miles's latest harassment target scuttle out the room. Not exactly a show of solidarity, but Esme understood the woman's need to escape. She'd been that woman for far too many years.

"Jealous—no. Sickened—definitely. I see you've dispensed with the five-year waiting period before you foist unwanted attentions on your employees. I really don't think they'll approve of cradle-robbing or harassment at corporate headquarters." She focused on staring him down, remembering the way Renzo had sent other men fleeing in the opposite direction the night they'd met at Club Paradise.

Unfortunately, the method didn't have the same immediate results. Miles reached for his steaming coffee mug labeled Executive Director, seemingly unaffected by her threat.

"I don't believe corporate will be too swayed by the opinions of troublemaking staffers who have been terminated." He sipped as he prowled the room, circling her like a hungry vulture.

Refusing to be cowed, Esme simply revealed the message she'd come here to deliver. "Maybe not. But once they have harassment complaints on file, I don't think they're going to keep buying the terminated-employee thing every time a mauled woman shows up at their doorstep. You might consider that before you bother any more of your assistants."

Pausing by the door to his office, Miles closed it and flicked the lock into place. "Maybe you're right. Lucky for me, it's not harassment if I target women who no longer work for the museum."

A niggle of panic washed over her. She assured herself she could still get out, however. The locked door merely meant other people couldn't get in.

All she needed to do was turn the knob and she could leave. Sleazebag Miles played these kinds of mind-game scare tactics simply to intimidate. Besides, he had the morning meeting to conduct soon and a museum full of staff a shout away.

She tilted her chin, steeled herself for the confrontation she'd been itching to have ever since he'd fired her. "You don't stand a chance of harassing me now. I'm not the same woman who walked out of here quietly six weeks ago."

He took a step closer, his footfall silenced by the thick Persian rug that covered his office floor. "Now that you mention it, you look a little different." His eyes roamed her body with far too much familiarity, her silk blouse and khaki skirt suddenly feeling inadequate.

He nodded thoughtfully as he perused, his nearness bringing a waft of cologne to her nose. "In fact, you look much better. Does that mean you came back here with your own designs for seduction?"

She'd forever associate that heavy scent with the feeling of being trapped. Only now she realized she had never been restrained by him so much as by her own fears.

"Hardly. It means I managed to find the courage to follow my own dreams instead of sitting around here waiting for you to notice my potential as an art historian." She didn't need Miles Crandall's endorsement to obtain another museum job. She had connections of her own—something that had given her an immediate strong client base for her work with Renzo.

Meeting him had lit a fire inside her in more ways than one. His vision and vitality had forced her to dream bigger, encouraged her to take chances she'd never imagined before.

"Then I suppose congratulations are in order. It seems I did you a favor by terminating you." Miles offered her his hand, as if they could shake and all would be healed between them. "Shall we let bygones be bygones?"

Esme would rather touch an electric eel than the viper in a three-piece suit in front of her.

"Actually, no. Just because I've found some happiness for myself doesn't mean I'm going to let you get away with railroading unsuspecting females who have the misfortune of working for you." She brushed past him and headed toward the door, his cologne giving her a headache while his mere presence made her want to lash out.

She paused just in front of the door, hand already on the knob. "I'm going to file complaints with our corporate parent, our sponsors and every state agency

I can think of to make sure your unprofessional be-
havior is well documented. I have the feeling you
won't be ruling the roost at the museum for much
longer, Miles. Enjoy it while it lasts."

Full of shaky adrenaline and pride, Esme flipped
open the lock to let herself out. She never heard Miles
approach until his hands braced the door shut, his
arms bracketing either side of her head.

His voice hissed in her ear. "I definitely plan to enjoy it. Thanks for making it possible."

Hands grabbed her, yanking her around and twisting her blouse in the process. Old Esme—that facet of
herself who had been raised not to take chances and to
hope no one disappointed you—hesitated for a split
second.

Long enough for Miles to slobber his way closer...as
if to kiss her?

New Esme didn't think twice about kneeing him in
the groin. Hard.

She packed every bit of frustration she'd ever had
working with the harassing creep into that blow, ren-
dering him doubled over and gasping for breath.

Not that she was sticking around to enjoy the victory or anything.

"Definitely not wise, Miles." She tugged open the
door to find the navy-suit-wearing brunette hovering
by the door, a heavy book hefted in one hand.

A weapon, maybe?

Esme pivoted on her heel. "And since I have a witness this time, you can be damn sure you'll be cooling your heels in the unemployment line by next week."

Winking at her silent, book-wielding partner, Esme stalked down the corridor with her pride flying high as she sought out the telephone to call the police.

RENZO SCANNED the building numbers along Bayshore Boulevard as he tore through traffic. Where the hell was that museum?

He'd been disappointed—even hurt, damn it—to wake up alone this morning. But that pang of deflated hope had been blown away by flat-out fear when he'd read Esme's note.

Seeing the building numbers grow closer to the museum address, Renzo let off the gas in his truck. Studied the street signs.

What had made her think she should confront her pervert ex-boss on her own this morning? Renzo had every intention of setting the guy straight today himself, but Esme had beat him to it while he slept in, dreaming about her, hoping he could find a way to break down those last barriers between them.

His tires squealed as he spied the building he sought and turned the truck into the parking lot. The old pickup didn't exactly turn on a dime.

If anything happened to her...

He couldn't even finish the thought. She'd gained so much confidence since he first met her. Soon she'd be walking all over him with her high heels and long skirts, her unapologetically feminine air mingled with a sharp mind and uncommon business sense.

If this former boss of hers did anything to jeopardize Esme's confidence, Renzo would rearrange his face personally.

Slamming the truck into park in the middle of the small lot, he slid out of the cab and made tracks for the side entrance. Barreling down a dark corridor toward a string of office doors lining the hallway, he nearly tripped over his own feet as Esme appeared in front of him, another woman close at her heels.

Renzo barely spared her friend a glance. And although somewhere in his mind's eye he saw Esme give him a crooked smile, the only thing he could fully grasp at the moment was her disheveled blouse and a big, fat bruise on the inside of her arm.

A bruise that sure as hell wasn't there yesterday.

Steam hissed through his veins, gaining momentum until it threatened to burst out his ears. Rage lodged in his throat, a tight knot of fury that inhibited his speech.

All he could manage was a rather choked, "Where. Is. He."

Esme took a step back, her expression concerned, her brows knit together. "I'm handling it. He's—"

Renzo didn't need to hear the rest because thankfully the silent brunette at her side pointed the way to the office door a few feet behind them.

And at this moment, with the image of Esme's

bruised skin blaring in his brain, that was all he needed to know.

"Renzo!" Esme called out to him, but he couldn't wait. Didn't know how to stop and listen until he'd cleaned this guy's clock.

For good.

Five steps later he spied his target. The guy leaned on his desk, sweating from his exertions and breathing heavy.

And didn't that just speak well of him?

Renzo's fists clenched automatically, but he only cocked one back before he planted it in the sweating pervert's face.

He didn't have a moment to take any satisfaction from the act however, because Esme's worried frown had turned into an all-out glare as she appeared in his line of vision.

Shouting.

"—and I already called the police. Are you crazy?" She stared at him with fury in her blue eyes and not the least bit of feminine gratitude.

The knot of rage that had been lodged in his throat slid down to his gut and twisted into a growing sickening feeling. The kind of nervous butterfly sensation that always kicks in when you've just done something stupid.

"The police?" Sirens already blared their way closer as Renzo realized what she was saying.

Esme really had taken care of this.

"Yes. But now instead of hauling off my would-be

attacker, they'll probably be hauling off the man throwing all the punches." Disappointment clouded her eyes. "Damn it, Renzo. Why couldn't you let me handle this my way?"

Because I was afraid you'd get hurt.

"Because this isn't a professional problem, this is a threat to your safety." Why couldn't she see that this wasn't about him being overbearing? She should have asked him to go with her this morning in the first place. "You made a bad decision to come here by yourself, Esme, admit it. It's one thing to buy a car on your own and another to have a face-off with a menace to society."

The sirens grew silent as a squad car pulled into the parking lot, lights flashing in a hypnotic rhythm through the office window of the perv eating carpet but still conscious at their feet.

"Point taken." Her words clipped, she tensed as the boots of at least two police officers clomped their way down the long corridor. "But by the time you arrived, I had it handled. Done. And the police were on the way. Would it have killed you to let me enjoy feeling like I took care of business on my own? Did it occur to you that maybe I needed this to be my victory?"

Her quiet honesty humbled him faster than any other woman's railing ever had. And hell yeah, he could understand her view.

"I was just so freaking mad when I walked in here—"

Esme's friend was already greeting the police while

her ex-boss made an effort to stand. She lowered her voice still further.

"Mad is fine. But I can't understand why you couldn't even be bothered to listen to me."

"How could I sit back and do nothing when you're walking around with your blouse half-torn off and a freaking bruise on your arm?" She was expecting too damn much of him. No Cesare would conscience seeing a woman disrespected like that. It was part of the genetic makeup.

"Because I wanted to work through this on my own. I told you that in the note I left you this morning and I told you last week that I was trying to find myself."

"Damn it, Esme, I would have listened to you about anything else. I know never to touch your television remote again. I didn't even tag along when you bought your new car. But this is different. I can't let you handle things by yourself if it means some harassing pervert is going to hurt you." How could he look himself in the mirror if he let anything happen to her?

By now the police were helping Esme's jack-off ex-boss into a chair. Any second they would be turning to him and Esme to ask them questions.

Esme shook her head, her blue eyes pinning him with unyielding determination. "And I can't work with someone who refuses to listen to me. While I'm grateful for the business opportunity you gave me, I think it's time for me to get back to my art history career. I have the feeling the museum will need a new executive director in the not-too-distant future. Besides, now that I've leveraged most of my contacts to inform them of your business, you'll be raking in plenty of sales without my help."

"Did it ever occur to you that this isn't about me needing to take charge?" Why couldn't she understand he was just scared out of his mind? "I was worried about you."

She tilted her jaw in a classic show of stubbornness. "You wouldn't have had to worry if you'd let me get a word in edgewise."

"Maybe this isn't the time to talk about this when we're both upset." He lowered his voice as the police approached them. "We could talk later—"

Unfazed by the arrival of a blue-uniformed audience, Esme shot back, "If you really want to talk, you're going to have to listen, too."

Before they could debate the issue, a stony-faced police officer interrupted them. Of course, while Renzo answered questions about his involvement in knocking Miles Crandall into yesteryear, he had plenty of time to come to the conclusion that Esme was giving him the boot—personally and professionally.

As he watched her answer questions and make her official statement to the police, Renzo saw even more evidence of her quiet strength and steely resolve. If he ran into this woman in Club Paradise today, he wouldn't be so quick to intercept her. She definitely didn't look like the kind of female who needed saving. Despite her delicate pink blouse and antique watch,

Esme possessed a new, level look in her blue eyes that said she could bring down the house if need be.

Well, damn.

What if he really had blown it for good with her this morning? Had he really been unforgivably high-handed this morning by giving Miles Crandall what he damn well deserved?

Not in his book. But he had to admit, maybe he wouldn't have been so quick to mete out his own brand of frontier justice if he'd known how important it was for Esme to kick the guy's tail herself.

Which, apparently he would have known if he'd been paying better attention for the past two weeks.

Unwilling to let her shut him out of her life because of one dumb-ass mistake, Renzo wracked his brain for a way to prove to her he could listen. How could he show her that, if he had to do it all over again, he could sit on his hands if she wanted him to?

By the time the police were finishing up their questions and—thank God—taking in this Crandall creep on a minor assault charge, Renzo had the beginnings of a plan in mind.

He just hoped Esme's matchmaking neighbor would be amenable to setting her up with the *right* guy this time.

14

BAD DECISION NUMBER five thousand forty, letting Mrs. Wolcott talk her into coming to Club Paradise tonight.

Esme steered her car into the line for valet parking and rued the moment she got sucked into a return visit to South Beach's hottest singles playground.

Of course, in the week since she'd told Miles Crandall where to get off and watched his sorry butt hauled off to jail for a night, Esme had made her fair share of good decisions, too. She'd come a long way from the woman determined to ignore her instincts and take a few risks since the last time she'd walked into the Moulin Rouge Lounge.

After mailing her notes on the antique business to Renzo and making sure he could find the staff to continue their work together, she'd taken over the executive director position at the South Florida museum since the corporate management ousted Miles. Next week marked her official triumphant return even though she'd already spent days redecorating her new office.

As Esme gave her car over to the valet and doled out a tip for the bellhop who would take her bags up to her suite, she wondered where she would snag a desk for the refurbished workspace.

It didn't seem right to accept Renzo's extravagant desk since she'd walked out of their new partnership and their fledgling relationship. But all week she kept envisioning that mammoth piece of furniture in the middle of the director's office.

A symbol of her strength, Renzo had called it.

Esme hesitated as she headed into the hotel entrance closest to the nightclub. The loner within begged her to proceed directly to the Sensualist's Suite and indulge in the free night's stay Pauline Wolcott had demanded Esme accept this time.

But new Esme—from now on, the *only* Esme— needed to make her way to the bar just to prove to herself she could. This time around she knew better than to snag any pre-poured glasses of champagne. And this time she knew better than to accept any blind dates.

Another one of her good decisions had been nixing that part of Mrs. Wolcott's plan. Esme had agreed to spend the night at the exotic hotel to celebrate her new job at the museum, but she drew the line when Pauline insisted Esme meet another blind date.

No thank you. Not this time.

Sexy Latin salsa music blared from the club's double doors as she made her way past the doorman and into the dimly lit interior of the bar. She didn't regret her wardrobe choice this time—a vintage black eyelet poet's shirt with well-worn jeans and strappy high heels. Her only real nod to evening wear were her painted pink toenails and the rhinestone costume jewelry she'd unearthed at a garage sale this morning.

Another good decision—not allowing anyone else's idea of fashion or beauty dictate her own style. Bra firmly in place, she felt comfortable in her own skin now.

Just more lonely than she'd ever been in her life.

And more than a little scared she'd made the wrong decision by taking the hard line with Renzo.

Weaving past drag queens and club kids through the dancing and strutting crowd, Esme ordered a Good Fortune Potion from a passing waitress and tried to tell herself she'd done the right thing by bailing out of a relationship with a take-charge forceful personality.

And actually, it probably would have been the right decision for Old Esme. Miss Geeky and Grateful could have never handled the kind of man who always thought he knew best and failed to consult other people for their opinions.

But in the wake of her big showdown with Miles at the museum, Esme kept thinking maybe now she could handle that kind of strong man. Something told her she'd given up too easily on a relationship that really might have gone somewhere. How could she have thrown in the towel when Renzo had probably only meant to help her? To protect her.

She'd been so quick to walk away because she'd been afraid of losing her newfound backbone. Yet now that she'd pulled her head together and vanquished a few personal demons, she couldn't imagine anything being strong enough to keep her down again.

Claiming a seat at a table in the back, Esme wondered how much longer she needed to linger in the Moulin Rouge Lounge in order to prove to herself that she could hit the nightclub scene without feeling like a total nerd. Five more minutes maybe?

Settling into a chair only a couple of yards away from where she and Renzo had sat a few weeks ago, Esme reached for her purse when her drink arrived.

Only it looked like...a beer?

Her gaze followed the imported long neck up to the broad masculine hand holding it, the muscular forearm leading to a strong chest, wide shoulders and buzz-cut blond hair.

"Brody?" She'd scarcely taken note of Renzo's employee last week because she'd been too wrapped up in her very own Stud of Italy, but she thought she recognized the cabinetmaker who'd been finishing a sideboard with Renzo's brother in the backyard.

The burly guy shuffled his feet, his cheeks clearly flushing even in the dim lights of the nightclub. "I was wondering if— That is, I hoped maybe you were looking for company?"

Surprised, Esme nudged the chair across from her with the toe of her high heel. "I'm only staying for a minute but have a seat."

Brody didn't sit.

He only looked more nervous as he shuffled again. "Actually I thought I'd see if you wanted to come back to my room with me." He tried for a half smile that looked more like a grimace. "If you like."

Surely she was missing something here. Renzo's employee showed up at Club Paradise to hit on her, only he didn't look like he was enjoying it very much.

"Pardon me?" Suspicious, Esme's gaze swept the room in search of the trick. For one thing, men rarely hit on her, and for another, poor Brody looked like he'd rather the ground open up to swallow him whole than have to repeat himself.

"I just wondered if you would come upstairs with me—"

"Wait." She rescued Brody from having to go through the whole spiel again when her gaze landed on a dark-eyed stud with an oh-so-familiar silhouette.

Lounging at a table a few yards away, Renzo Cesare watched her every move, literally sitting on his hands while she fended for herself in Miami's most notorious pick-up joint.

Laughter tickled her throat, teased a smile free in spite of herself. It wasn't easy to stay mad at a man with a sense of humor.

He raised his bottle of water to her in silent toast, his eyes never leaving hers.

A tingle of anticipation shivered through her, a rogue wave of wishfulness she couldn't afford to indulge.

Brody took a step back, the movement of his big

body distracting her. "Maybe I ought to just say good-night."

Esme rose to kiss him on the cheek. "Sorry you were coerced into that," she whispered in his ear, thinking she knew the ideal woman for this quiet, sweet and totally gorgeous younger man. "If you ever find yourself between girlfriends you ought to drop by the South Florida museum sometime. My new assistant director is a little bit shy, but if that doesn't bother you—"

"It doesn't." He couldn't jump on the invitation fast enough. "And I just happen to be between girlfriends right now."

Smothering a laugh, Esme handed him a crisp new business card with the museum's address on it. "Then stop in any time."

She'd barely finished the sentence when her feminine radar sensed Renzo's intense, interested gaze on her. Peering over her shoulder as Brody doled out grateful thanks, Esme found her former business partner still sitting on his hands, but he craned his neck to keep them in his sights.

Her heart clenched, skipped a beat at the notion that he had tracked her down here tonight. After sending Brody on his way, Esme caught her waitress and retrieved her Good Fortune Potion before following her feet to Renzo's table.

The magnetic pull of the man drew her close before she could even calculate the proper boundaries. She stopped a mere foot away, staring down into the fathomless dark eyes that had captured her imagination from that very first night.

"I had to come over to see what prompted you to torture poor Brody into hitting on me tonight." So maybe she already had a good idea why. Her injured pride wanted a little reassurance.

Renzo slid his water bottle onto the table and rose, his full height right next to her igniting a small flame in her heart.

"Brody might be a quiet guy, but trust me, he didn't look at hitting on you as torture. I guarantee you if you'd shown the least bit of interest in his proposition, he would have been swinging from the rafters."

It wasn't the response she'd expected, but his words still made her smile. "Nevertheless, I don't think he would have approached me tonight if you hadn't asked him to."

"Maybe I wanted you to know that I think you can handle yourself. That I can rein in my impulses to give you room to do things your own way."

"And what would you *really* have done if I'd taken Brody up on his offer?" Not that she would have in a million years since the only man she wanted to be with was standing right in front of her. "Because I'm not buying the rafters notion."

He swallowed hard. "Honestly, I would have wanted to knock Brody into the next millennium, but I realize now that wouldn't gain me a damn thing but sore knuckles. Instead, I probably would have settled for getting sloppy drunk and landing on my sister's doorstep to pour out my broken heart."

Esme melted a little. "Broken heart?"

He reached to touch her, his hand looming close to her cheek just as a rowdy group of newcomers stumbled off the dance floor to raid the minibar near them.

The mood broken, Renzo nodded toward the exit. "Do you have a few minutes to take this outside? We could talk where it's quiet." He paused. "Talk *and* listen."

He leaned closer, a hint of his aftershave teasing her nose while the heat of his body teased the rest of her. The light, sexy scent of him was so much different than the suffocating fumes Miles had worn. Funny that she'd found the gumption to confront Miles, but she seemed to still be running from Renzo.

What had she been thinking to allow herself to be intimidated by life? Sure, falling for him was scary, but she could handle it.

She loved him.

Renzo's voice whispered through her thoughts as his lips moved against her ear. "The hotel sits on a beautiful stretch of beach."

She stared up into his dark eyes and wondered why she would say no to this man anyway. For all the trouble his take-charge ways could cause, his strength of personality also pushed her out of her comfort zone, encouraged her to take chances.

And suddenly, strolling on a warm beach at midnight with a gorgeous man by her side sounded very appealing.

At her nod, Renzo slid his hand around hers, drew her forward through the crowd behind his big body. The sea of club-goers parted for him, and Esme thought there could be worse things than to have a man in your life who would occasionally clear your path.

As long as it wasn't *all* the time. As long as he could understand that sometimes she needed to forge her own way.

Exiting the club, he steered her around a corridor into the hotel and then out through double doors leading outside. The moist ocean air and salty scent of the wind assailed her senses, a soothing contrast to the urgent pulse of funky hip-hop music that had been playing in the bar.

The gentle, sultry breeze reminded Esme of their twilight walk through the Vizcaya gardens. She'd been so daring that night, bolder than ever before.

Renzo started for a pair of beach loungers drawn up close together, then paused. Pivoted on his heel to face her. "Do you want to sit, or do you want to head down to the water?"

It was a simple thing, his consulting her on this small issue. Still, Esme knew three weeks ago he would have simply led them where he wanted.

Bending to slide out of her high heels, Esme nodded toward the dark expanse of ocean dotted with a hand-

ful of tiny lights emanating from boats on the horizon.
"Let's live on the edge."

He quirked a thick, dark eyebrow in her direction
and then scooped up her shoes.

They stepped off the deck and into the sand. Renzo
seemed impervious to the soft grain in his boat shoes
with no socks. Esme relished the feel of the groomed
beach beneath her toes.

The sound of lapping water against the shore grew
louder as they neared the incoming tide. Esme side-
stepped a forgotten volleyball in the sand before
Renzo kicked it back toward the hotel so it wouldn't
wash out to sea.

"So you weren't up for a blind date tonight?" He
halted a few feet from the surf, his voice riding the
salty breeze to her ears while her eyelet blouse rippled
against her skin.

"What do you mean?" She leaned over to pick up a
smooth shell half buried in the sand. He couldn't possibly know about the blind date Mrs. Wolcott had suggested to her this weekend.

"I asked your matchmaking neighbor to see if she
could set me up with you for real this time, but she
told me afterward that you couldn't be swayed." He
set her shoes a few feet away from them, safe from the
encroaching water.

"*You* were the date Pauline was angling for?" Her
sneaky neighbor definitely had a romanticized view
of love. Hard to believe anyone could be so relent-

lessly optimistic after a handful of divorces, but Esme had to admire the woman's ability to take a chance.

He nodded, his shadowed expression illuminated by moonlight. "She also told me about your promotion at the museum. Congratulations."

"Thank you." In the past, she would have shrugged off praise for her accomplishments. Now, she wanted to bask just a little, enjoy the milestones. "I can't believe you asked Pauline to set us up."

"She served me tea by the gallon and quizzed me about any male in my family over fifty. I think she might be in the market for another husband."

Laughing, Esme decided to keep an eye out for bachelor prospects for Mrs. Wolcott. "She's a sweet person, but she told me it's taken her fifty years to grow up."

Esme hadn't known what to make of that comment at the time, but just now, hanging out in the moonlight with Renzo, she knew she didn't want to spend her whole life figuring out who she wanted to be.

She wanted to start living now. Tonight.

Renzo watched Esme carefully wash the sand off a shell and prayed he could convince this cautious woman that he was the right man for her.

He'd been too inflexible—and maybe a little unwilling—to change for Celeste. Obviously, he hadn't loved her the way he loved Esme because something about Esme's steely, quiet strength and undemanding character made him want to change for her.

Or at least *try*.

He wasn't willing to give up on Esme.

"You know why I wanted the date tonight?" He took the clean shell out of her hand, depositing it into the pocket of his shirt so he could touch her, hold her. He rested his fingers on her shoulders, forced himself not to rush this.

"You were hoping I'd mistake you for someone else and drag you off to bed again?" Her blue eyes glinted with humor even in the dark.

"Okay, call me arrogant all you want, but I'm sure as hell hoping if I'm ever fortunate enough to find myself in your bed again it will be because you know exactly who I am." He allowed his fingers to curve around her shoulders, to slide underneath the veil of her hair. "Esme, I wanted to see you again so I could tell you how sorry I am for not having a clue last week and tromping all over your big moment. If I had to do it all over, I swear I'd find a way to keep my fists to myself and cheer you on from the sidelines."

"Yeah?" She gave a careless shrug, yet Renzo could feel the race of her heart, the urgent thump of her pulse through her delicate body. "You know, half the reason you were able to knock him out so fast was because I'd just kneed him in the, um...groin...five seconds before that. He barely survived me."

Renzo smiled, partly at the image of petite Esme kicking butt and partly just because she looked so damn proud. "I figured somebody must have softened him up for me."

He wanted to draw her close and kiss her, but he

wouldn't be able to stand it if she pulled away. Besides, he hadn't said nearly everything he needed to.

Clearing his throat, he dove into the heart of the problem. "You know, I can't promise you that I won't occasionally act before I think. But if you'd ever agree to give us a second chance, I can promise you I will always try and listen."

"You would?" She swiped away a windblown strand of hair in her eyes. "Because even though I feel more confident in who I am and what I want these days, I'll never be the kind of woman who shouts out what she needs or gets in your face to make sure you know what's important to me."

His heart squeezed painfully with her words, giving him just a small taste of what he would feel like if Esme turned him down tonight.

"Honey, you could whisper what you want, and I swear to you I'll go stone-cold silent to hear what you have to say."

One corner of her beautiful mouth hitched up. "Really?"

And was it his imagination, or did he catch a wicked glint in her eye?

He crossed his heart, snagging his finger on the shell in his shirt pocket. "Promise."

"Then maybe I shouldn't be so quick to run at the first sign of trouble." She inclined her head to his chest, her silky hair tickling his chin. "That's a promise I'll make you in return."

Surely he'd never been given such a big gift in his

whole life. His train set when he was ten couldn't even come close to the magnitude of Esme's trust.

The stranglehold on his heart eased as his blood started flowing again, his whole world opening up with new possibilities.

"I love you, Esme."

She wrenched her gaze up, startled.

He wound his arms around her, determined not to let her go. Not mess this up. "I've never met anyone I don't have to shout at to make a point. My whole family talks so much we have to yell just to hear one another. And guys on a construction crew—hell—we take great pride in voice projection and creative cursing. But it's a totally new experience for me to just talk to you and have you really listen."

Tears built in Esme's eyes, convincing him he'd overplayed his hand. Why the hell couldn't he have waited to heap on his undying love? The poor woman would be running away screaming soon while he and his need to blurt out everything nursed the worst broken heart in Cesare history.

"I messed this up, didn't I?" He swiped away one fat tear with his thumb.

Shaking her head, she loosened more tears to trail down her soft cheeks. "No. I just can't believe that taking a chance could have such a fast, amazing payback."

Renzo ducked to kiss her, taste her tears, her sweet lips and his future.

Her arms coiled around his neck as she stepped

closer. Between kisses she murmured in his ear, "I love you, too."

He hauled her up in his arms, just enough to spin her around, his feet kicking up soft sand while he whirled her through the air.

She laughed. Squealed. Kissed him again until he was senseless from spinning and imagining a future with kick-butt Esmerelda Giles at his side.

"Now that we have that settled, can you tell me how I can make you agree to marry me?" Renzo knew that with Esme's determined nature, if she said yes now, no power on earth could make her not show up at the altar. "Maybe we can elope and skip the whole noisy family deal. We can do something quiet and romantic and—" He stopped himself midstream, remembering his promise to listen. "Wait. What would you like to do for a wedding? That is, if you care to accept my proposal."

"Oh, I most definitely accept." Sliding to her feet, she poked him in the ribs, her lips full and soft from his kisses. "But eloping is out of the question. Since I've never had much family to speak of, I intend to soak up the whole brother-sister experience as soon as possible."

"You have no clue what you're in for." But secretly, he was glad as all get-out that she wanted to be a part of his family, that she wasn't afraid to wade into relationships with his noisy, boisterous clan.

She smiled that gentle, knowing Esme grin that made him realize who would always be the real head of the household no matter how much he shouted or steamrolled his way through life.

"I'm hoping it will be a lifetime of love and compromise and family."

Family.

The word took on new and improved meaning when Esme said it like that, with the secretive smile on her face.

"Didn't your neighbor reserve you a room here for the night?" He suddenly couldn't wait to get her alone. "We could get a head start on that whole family deal."

"Only if you promise me no more talk of eloping."

"Done." He retrieved her shoes and scooped her off her feet, already wondering where he could build her the perfect house. "And I'm going to carry you over the threshold on our wedding day just like this. I can build a house in six months flat, you know. A good one, too. And you'll have all kinds of decisions to make—choosing the right bed, the best bedroom furniture, all the sexy extras like a hot tub..." He couldn't wait to get started.

Heading back toward the hotel, he savored the best night of his life with his bride to-be in his arms.

"That will be nice," she admitted. "But right now I'm more concerned with one thing."

He paused, remembering his promise to listen.

Leaning closer, she whispered in his ear. "Make love to me."

And to hell with walking, Renzo took off for her hotel room at a dead run.

Epilogue

Esmerelda Cesare admired the lace tulle of her vintage wedding gown and wondered how she'd ever managed so much good luck.

Twirling in front of the mirror in the ladies' lounge just outside of Club Paradise's biggest ballroom where her wedding reception was now in progress, she admitted the heirloom gown had been the perfect wardrobe choice for her big day. She'd been incredibly fortunate to find a man who loved her to distraction, and thanks to her wealth of generous new family members, she had also lucked into wearing the dress Renzo's mother had worn when she married his father thirty-six years before. The garment had not only been a perfect fit, it also struck her as incredibly romantic and made her feel like part of the family.

"You look like a dream!" Renzo's sister, Giselle appeared in the mirror behind her. An exotic, dark-eyed beauty with olive skin and scads of long brown hair, Giselle looked amazing in a simple, icy-pink sheath dress. "My father would have loved to see one of his sons' brides wear my mother's dress. He would have nearly burst with pride."

"I just hated to steal it out from under you, Giselle." Esme had fretted about that from the start. "It seemed like you should be the one walking down the aisle in it."

"Bite your tongue." Giselle batted Esme's arms with her pink satin purse. "Not only would this body fail to fit in a tiny size, like negative two, under any conditions, I also have every intention of remaining single."

She fished in her purse for her shiny coral lipstick and slicked on a new coat while Esme monitored her upswept hairdo for stray pieces.

"I never thought I would marry either." Until her orderly life had swerved out of control and she'd met Renzo, Esme had been perfectly content to bury herself in work and insulate herself from the emotional highs and lows inevitable in relationships. Now, she would never trade passion for predictability again. "But when you meet the right person, all bets are off."

Giselle stuffed her lipstick back in her bag and then fluffed Esme's short train. "Marriage is fine for you lovey-dovey types, but I plan to play the field once I can wriggle out from under my brothers' thumbs. In fact," she lowered her voice as if for dramatic effect. "I predict lots of sensual mayhem while you two are on your honeymoon."

Esme smiled to herself as she practically floated back out to the packed reception hall of family and friends. Giselle's fellow Club Paradise co-owners partied at their own table along with a prominent state legislator who was somewhat of a local celebrity. Only the Club Paradise CEO Lainie Reynolds was absent.

She apparently had some sort of old beef with Giselle and had taken a business trip in order to politely bow out of the happy event.

Finally, Esme spied Renzo who stood with his back to her, surrounded by his bevy of brothers and some hundred and twenty guests. Immediately, her body responded to the sight of her new husband in a tuxedo and tie, the crisp black lines of his jacket accentuating the breadth of his shoulders and the V of his back down to lean hips. Yum.

Although it had been four months since they got engaged and they'd gotten to know one another very intimately on a regular basis since then, they'd decided to turn abstinent for ten days before the wedding so they would appreciate their first night as husband and wife all the more.

Five days into the experiment, she'd decided they were never spending ten days apart again. Ever.

He turned as she approached, perhaps picking up on her deluge of provocative thoughts. "Are you ready to cut the cake? Nico here is going to start drooling in it if we don't feed him a piece soon."

Sure enough, all three of Renzo's brothers hovered about the table where Giselle's gorgeous confection resided. Vito, the oldest Cesare who had raised his siblings after their father died, was already wielding the wedding knife and a silver spatula decorated with orange blossoms. Quieter than his rowdy brothers, Vito possessed a hungry intensity that seemed to fit a man hell-bent on winning every trophy the European racing circuit had to offer.

Nico seemed to be using his skills from his hockey days to elbow back the competition from the cake table. Plate in hand, he nudged Marco—the youngest who was home from Harvard on spring break—out of the running.

And no wonder. The cake was pure fairy tale with its four tiered layers of white frosted perfection. Real pansy petals decorated the plate while tiny purple frosted flowers decorated the tiers.

"Maybe it's just me," Renzo whispered for her ears alone as he drew her close. His family was distracted for the moment as they tried to keep Marco and Nico from wrestling. "But don't those flowers look sort of provocative? The way the petals fold make me think of—"

"Don't say it." She knew exactly what he was thinking because she'd thought it, too, when she'd first seen the cake. "I'm sure Giselle would never plant erotic images on our wedding cake. It's just because we've got sex on the brain."

Renzo shot his sister a dark glare that fell short of being ominous because her new husband was so obviously happy. Giselle winked back, all innocent smiles while she poured herself another glass of champagne from the decorative mountain of elegant green bottles on the cake table.

Maybe Giselle hadn't been kidding about a week of

sensual mayhem while Renzo was out of town on his honeymoon.

Vito finally held up a quieting hand to rein in the crowd. "Show a little respect for the bride," he ordered his brothers, passing Esme the wedding knife with a flourish. "This is her show, not ours."

Amid much flashbulb popping and laughter, Esme and Renzo managed to cut their cake and feed one another bites of the vanilla-and-almond-flavored confection. Esme's heart caught in her throat as Renzo wiped the frosting from her lips with the pad of his thumb, his eyes devouring hers. Goose bumps shivered over her skin, tingling nerves inside and out.

The big-band style musicians kicked up again as Giselle skillfully cut cake and passed plates to the small army of Cesare family relatives who had attended the wedding. Esme claimed only her mother, a few school friends and museum staffers, including her assistant with the grinning Brody on her arm. Mrs. Wolcott played mother of the bride whenever Esme's mom felt too shy, easily making sure the guests were seated in the right places and that the band played at the right times.

She'd been too busy to take note of all the Italian uncles, but maybe later...

"Want to dance?" Renzo's voice broke through her contented reverie, his deep rumble igniting all the little butterflies of anticipation again.

Esme set aside the remnants of her cake to find her way into his arms.

"I can't believe we're married." She stared up into his eyes, twining one hand around his shoulder while the chandelier lights glinted on his dark hair. How had everything happened so fast?

"You're going to love the new house." He'd had a construction crew working on their small plot of land in Coral Gables nonstop for months. Luckily, now that their antique reproduction business was flourishing, they'd been able to afford some overtime to pay the guys who were putting everything together in time for when they returned from an extended honeymoon in Rome.

"Definitely. Although I might love having you at my beck and call for the next month even more." She allowed her fingers to stray down his chest, to smooth his lapel and dip onto the cotton of his shirt.

"Not a wise move if you want to enjoy the rest of your wedding day." His stern warning sounded just a little strangled.

She moved in closer to appreciate the feel of his body next to hers. "Maybe I'm just getting ready to enjoy the wedding night."

Renzo tipped his forehead to hers, his eyelids falling shut. "A few more dances and we'll go. I'm dying to get you all to myself."

Esme smiled to think she wasn't the only one suffering from desire overload. She wanted him so bad her ears were ringing with it.

No, wait.

Her ears were ringing because one hundred and

twenty wedding guests were clanging on their tea-cups and champagne glasses with their silverware.

"Looks like we've at least earned permission to kiss." She paused as they danced, her world of orange blossoms and happy family narrowing until all she could see was Renzo.

Definitely the man of her dreams.

Her heart thudded heavy in her chest as he slanted his mouth over hers for a kiss that sent the whole re-ception hall howling.

Joy bubbled inside Esme along with a hefty dose of passion for her new husband.

And she realized she'd just committed excellent de-cision number one—tying the knot with her very own Stud of Italy.

* * * * *

SINGLE IN SOUTH BEACH *is returning!*
Look for the night life to heat up once again
in May 2004 in Harlequin Blaze as
Joanne Rock takes us back to Club Paradise.

And be sure to catch Joanne's Harlequin
Historical debut in February 2004 with
THE WEDDING KNIGHT where she
shows that hot nights are timeless...